Dedication

This book is dedicated to my very own Trilogy; my PARENTS whose love & support has helped me get this far, my HUSBAND who has never once given up on me and always pushing me even at times when I wanted to give up, and to my son SKYLAR, without you this story would have never been told. Thank You! You all taught me to never give up, never surrender and let your journey to your dreams & goals take you far.

You're Never Too Old To Chase Your Dreams...

C. A. Poptanberry

Copyright © 2014 by C.H Fortenberry, Carla H. Fortenberry
All rights reserved. No part of this book may be reproduced, scanned or distributed in any printed or electronic form without permission.
Simms Books
Published by Simms Books Publishing
2014
ISBN 978-0-692-30318-4
Printed in United States of America
Book design By Ana Cruz @ Ana Cruz Arts, R. Jenkins @Innovativedesignstyle.Com
Interior layout by Nidia Roman @ Romanarts
Transcribed by Judy Hattaway
Edited by Danielle Reed @Reedwrites

ACKNOWLEDGEMENTS

There are so many people I need to thank. Just where do I begin? I first want to thank God for giving me the most vivid dreams and imagination I could ever ask for. That's how my stories all begin, through my dreams.

I want to thank my parents, especially my mom for being my "pre-editor" so that when my story was complete and in the hands of the real editors, they wouldn't look at me as crazy because of all my misspelled words and horrendous sentence structure.

I want to thank my cover Artist Ana Cruz of Ana Cruz Art and Rebekah Jenkins of Innovative Design Style, for taking a great cover and making it spectacular! Ana you were able to get in my crazy head and give my character Murranda (Murry) a face. Thank you Nidia Roman of RomanArts for interpreting my vision of The Rose and coming up with perfect chapter art work that made me cry. I hope to work with you all for a long time and you all are truly amazing artist!

To my editor, Danielle Reed @ Reedwrites, thank you for being so patient with this new writer and for helping me bring my story to life.

To James R. Simms my publishing guru at Simms Books Publishing, you helped make my dream of becoming an author come true. To my PR girl, my motivator, Kathleen P. Martin at ThroughKatzEyezMedia.com and MadameKatCeo on Blog Talk Radio, thanks for all your guidance and showing me the light to step into to shine.

To my friends, My Dream Team, Dee, Cozmo, Murry, Lisa, Keith, Jamie, Jessica, Jett, Vanessa, Jason B., John M, Matthew, Janet, and DGS,

ExpressJet and anyone else I may have forgotten to name thanks for putting up with me always talking about my book and bouncing crazy ideas off of you.

Thanks to my AMAZING HUSBAND for being patient and NEVER giving up on me even when I wanted to give up on myself. You just kept pushing. THANK YOU! Thanks to my son SKYLAR, for without you this book would never have been written. You gave my story life. This just proves that with hard work and great support team you too can reach your dreams.

Finally last but certainly not least, Thank you Sharon Robinson. You gave me a card that would change my life, James R. Simms's card when I mentioned I was working on a book. You handed me the key to my new journey and I will forever be grateful to you. Thank you.

To all the readers and dreamers out there who is reading this book. THANK YOU! For helping to make my dreams come true. You are never too old to dream, Remember IMAGINATION HAS NO AGE LIMIT! I hope you like what you read, tell others about it and continue with me on my journey and series.

CHAPTER 1

Once, long, long ago, there was a land called Xeenoephillia. This was a land full of mystery, magic, and adventure.

In this land, unicorns and dragons battled forces, mermaids swam with dolphins and dreamed of walking on land. Kings and Queens ruled this kingdom, while wizards and sorcerers cast their many spells.

While most of the land was happy, there also existed a dark part of this world; a place where one might encounter vampires, werewolves and other creatures of the night. This was a land where Good and Evil met. Here existed mystical creatures—inhuman beings and mortals alike.

If you were to come upon this land, one might see elves and fairies dancing around or causing mischief, and, if you were lucky, you might even find a leprechaun or two.

In another part of this world you could wander upon Indians gathered around a bonfire listening to their chiefs and medicine men speaking about the old days and the animal spirits that would guide them. You might even come in contact with a pirate ship carrying a band of drunken seadogs singing songs. But let's not get too far ahead.

First let me tell you a little about myself. My name is Murranda Lyn Delarenzo—known to my friends and family as Murry. I am 18. I have lived in this world I have described to you my entire life. I live in a big, beautiful house with acres of land stretching for miles with an equally beautiful lake along the eastern border of our land.

My father, Count Rudolpho Delarenzo who most know as Rudy, raised me. He is a tall and very well built man with sun kissed skin, short, sleek, jet-black hair and dark brown eyes. He has grown a thin goatee and his dimples show when he smiles. I look a lot like my father, except I got my mother's coral blue eyes.

Being the daughter of a well-known count, you can imagine my room is filled with the finest things money can buy—a queen size canopy bed, draped with the finest silks and beads; an arched window overlooking the lake. The window seat is filled with pillows. On one side of my room, a huge walk-in closet with the finest clothes money can buy. Even though I prefer wearing what my father would consider boy's clothes sewn by our seamstress. My father has always insisted I dress up and look more like a young lady. Much to his chagrin I always manage to find ways to get back into my pants and blouses.

On the other side of my room I have a red couch facing a small stage that I created. Since I was very small, I have loved to entertain my family and friends with music, songs and dance. I was taught to play many different instruments including the piano, guitar, flute, violin and harp.

My favorite instrument is an old guitar that once belonged to my mother. I carry it around with me everywhere I go. I used to say it made me feel as though Mother was right with me when I played it. My mother, Countess Morinda Lyn Delarenzo died after giving birth to me.

My mother was a very beautiful woman who was loved by everyone. She was a petite woman with tan skin, and unusually deep blue, slanted eyes. She also had a beauty mark on her outer upper lip that was shaped like a tiny star. I got that too.

Even though I was a newborn when my mother died, I know much about her because of the stories my father has told me. Every night at bedtime my father would enthrall me with tales of their love for one another, and recall the dreams and many adventures they'd shared. I know he loved her very much.

I love listening to those stories. I even keep a picture of my mother on the nightstand by my bed. I also wear a half locket necklace with my mother's picture in it. Mother was buried with the other half, which holds my baby picture.

I often dream about the stories my father has told me. I can almost picture every word, every detail. One morning, I awoke from one of my dreams with an intense feeling I couldn't explain. It troubled me deeply, but unsure of what to do, I tried to ignore the feeling. I got out of bed and got ready for breakfast with my father.

I left my room dressed in a pair of dark pants and a multi colored blouse.

As I walked down the hallway, I stopped to admire the paintings hanging along the wall. There was one of my grandparents, and one of my Uncle Leo. He had been a dashing and brave noble knight to the King and Queen. There was also my most favorite painting of all—the one of my mother and father's wedding.

My mother, Morinda, was standing with the most beautiful white gown that sparkled with diamonds. She had tiny orchids in her hair and was holding a bouquet of light purple orchids and pink roses. My father was standing with his arm around her looking very regal in his suit. Next to the wedding portrait was a statue of Mother holding a baby girl I knew to be me.

I continued walking through the hall and down the winding staircase. I ran down to meet father in the dining room.

We had a huge dining room with a crystal chandelier and a marble floor. It was big enough for grand balls and other events that we've had, but for today, there was simply a single long table in the middle of the room plated with the family china.

Father was sitting at one end of the table reading his paper. He stood when he noticed me. I ran to him and gave him a big hug and a kiss.

Father eyed me, "Murranda! I really wish you would dress more appropriately for meals." he said

"Oh Father!" I rolled my eyes and replied

I sat at the other end of the table. Jeffery, our family's butler for many years, came and asked what I would like for breakfast.

"Mmm, I hope I am smelling what I think, Jeffery. Did the chef make his famous wild blueberry pancakes?"

"Yes, he did my lady. Would you like some with some juice and coffee?"

"Yes, I would. Thank you."

Father had his usual: a cup of coffee and eggs Benedict. He watched me as I ate—I knew he sensed my discomfort.

"What is troubling you Sunshine? You look as if you are carrying the whole world on your shoulders."

"I am alright Father. Well, sort of."

I did not know how to tell him what was wrong when I really wasn't sure of what it was myself.

"I just feel like I am missing something, something that I must have and need to find."

He looked puzzled and asked, "What can you be looking for when you have everything you could ever want or dream of."

I got up from the table and walked over to sit down next to him and hold his hand. "That is the problem Father. I don't know what it is that I need to find. I just know deep inside my heart that I have to find this thing no matter how long it takes or where it takes me."

He stood up from the table and with a stern voice, asked "What do you mean how long it takes or where it takes you. What are you trying to tell me Sunshine? I have already lost your mother, the love of my life, my shining star, and now you think I am going to just let YOU leave me, not just NO, but I forbid it." He yelled with tears in his eyes.

"You don't even know what it is you're missing!"

"Why are you acting this way Father? I am not a little girl any more. I am at the age of marriage. I can make my own choices. You need to let me go. I promise to return as soon as I find what I am looking for."

"And how long will that take?" he asked. "You don't even know what 'it' is. Plus you have never been away from home or from me before. You will be all alone."

I stood up and looked deep into his eyes. "We both knew this day would come Father. My mother gave me the breath of life when she gave up her own, and you raised me and gave me wings. Through your love and her love, I know I will be fine. Now it's time to let me go."

He looked into my eyes seeing his beloved wife through the tears of desperation in his own. He gently kissed my forehead and said, "You look so much like your mother now."

He took a deep breath, let it out slowly and continued, "I could never say no to your mother, so I guess we need to get you ready for your journey. Before you leave me alone in this big house, would you please help me with your mother's garden? Her birthday is coming. You must know how much she loved her garden."

After breakfast, we walked out onto the patio to the garden. It was a perfect place—just the right amount of sunlight and shade and a space in the corner to sit and enjoy it. Father always told me that my mother and I were a lot alike. We both loved flowers, and even though we had servants responsible for the grounds, we enjoyed doing our own gardening.

Mother and I also shared a love of stories and we both kept diaries. In fact, I found my mother's last diary. It told about the dream garden she wanted for her 40th birthday. Even though she was gone, we both wanted to make her last dream a reality, so that when she looked down from Heaven she could see her dream come to life.

While Father was working the soil, he asked me to go into town and buy as many beautiful flowers as I could, as well as anything else we might need for the garden. He also said to purchase anything I would need for my journey. While he worked, the servants hitched the horses to the wagon and I headed into town.

I loved our village. Everyone knew one another and the people were very friendly. It did not matter if you were wealthy or not. There were a few of the upper class who thought themselves better than others, but for the most part we all got along.

In town, there were many shops and street vendors where you could find anything you needed at whatever price you could afford to pay. As I approached the main street, I could hear the church bells and smell the various aromas of the stores and street stalls. The poor orphan children looked longingly into the bakery window where the pies, bread and other wonderful goodies were placed. On some of my trips into town I would stop and buy a few goodies for them, but, today I did not stop.

As I approached the center of town, I noticed a sign that I had never seen before. It read, FANTASY GARDEN.

Well, that looks interesting, I thought, to no one in particular. *I wonder what types of flowers and plants they carry.* I decided to go in and have a look around.

When I entered, I couldn't believe my eyes. The sight, smells, colors, and sounds took my breath away. I felt as though I had stepped into a garden paradise.

There were all species of flowers—familiar ones, such as roses, daisies, orchids, daffodils, lilacs, jasmine and even sunflowers as big as your head. Others were beyond my imagination.

I saw flowers that changed colors on their own and some that would change colors depending on who was holding the flower and the person's mood at the time. There were flowers that played music. Some flowers would dance while others sparkled and glittered. Some would shoot off tiny fireworks. There were even flowers that could talk.

Then, to my amazement, I noticed fairies flying around and little elves taking care of the flowers.

"How can I help you?" said a tiny voice.

I looked around and saw nothing. Then I felt something, or someone, tugging at my pants leg. I looked down and there near the floor, was a tiny fairy.

"Oh my!" I said, leaning in to pick it up, "You are so small. Why aren't you flying like the others?"

As I sat the tiny thing in my hand, I noticed that one of its wings was tangled in a spider's web.

"Oh, I see. Let me help you out of this, and we'll see if you can then help me."

I took a small handkerchief from my bag and found a bottle of water next to one of the plants, and proceeded to wipe off the web from the fairy's wing.

"Oh thank you kind lady. Thank you very much."

He giggled and laughed while I removed the sticky parts. Then when his wings were cleared he fluttered around me.

"My name is Glitz," he said.

"Nice to meet you Glitz. My name is Murranda," He flitted and fluttered around my ears and head. "If you would hold still, I might be able to see you better and talk to you," I said, squinting my eyes to look for him.

"Oh bother, I can fix that," he said.

He raised his hands in the air and pointed his feet toward the ground. I could see him getting taller and taller until he was the size of a small child with wings.

Now that he was closer to human size, I could see he had a very childlike face with dirty blond hair and hazel eyes. He was dressed in what appeared to be leaves sewn together in hues of dark green and golden. He wore a rope-like belt with a pouch attached to one side and a pan flute attached to the other. His feet were bare, and his wings were similar to dark green leaves. His skin was fair, but dirty, and he was spattered with freckles. When he smiled you could see a tiny gap between his teeth.

"WOW! I didn't know fairies could grow like that!" I said, surprised.

"Oh yes. All fairies can do that. Although we prefer to stay tiny…easier to fly. But we're able to grow this big. It helps when we're around you mortals. We wouldn't want you to mistake us for flies and give us a swat." Glitz giggled. "So, how can I help you today, Murranda?"

I looked around the plant nursery. "Well, my father and I are planting a huge garden in honor of my mother's birthday. We are in need of some of your wonderful and exotic flowers."

"This must be a really big garden," Glitz said. "You've come to the right place. I guess we should get started."

We walked around the plant nursery. I noticed other fairies, elves, and even some wood nymphs working. All the different and unique flowers amazed me. If you wanted just the flowers, you could pick them, but if you wanted to plant them at your home, you would need the seeds. I selected a dozen of every flower seed I recognized.

In the meantime, Glitz and the other fairies and elves gathered the unusual flowers; ones that would sparkle and glittered, some of the singing ones and a few color changers. As I turned a corner to see the dancing flowers I heard tiny voices saying, "What about us? We want to be in your garden."

Startled, I turned around and saw what appeared to be calla lilies with faces. I walked over and knelt beside one of them.

"Did you just say something?"

There was no reply. "Mmm I guess not. I must be hearing things," I said, blushing as I stood to walk away.

"That depends on if you will add us to your garden." said the flower.

"Aha! You can talk!" I shouted pointing my finger.

"Don't you know it's rude to point," scolded one of the flowers with a tiny stern voice.

"Oh, I am so sorry," I replied picking up a few calla lilies, "but, but...it's just...well, you can talk."

"Of course, we can talk. How else could we let you know what we're feeling?"

I walked toward the front counter, seeds and calla lilies in hand when I noticed a room in the corner with a sign reading, *Make Your Own Flower*. Now, I was really intrigued.

I asked if they would hold my things at the counter and made my way toward the corner flower room. I could see sparks and dusty smoke coming through the bottom of the door.

Suddenly, a wood nymph exited the room carrying a tiny fairy on her shoulder. The nymph was tall and slender with red hair. She was wearing a green gauzy dress with shiny gold glitter scattered throughout and she wore no shoes. The little fairy on her shoulder was very young, with shiny green wings so sheer you could almost see through them.

"Hi there. You must be Murranda, the flower child. The whole nursery is talking about you," said the nymph.

"Flower child? Talking about me? Why?" I asked.

"Oh excuse my manners," said the nymph. "My name is Dee Dee and this is my friend Flutter."

The young fairy darted shyly behind Dee Dee "Flutter is a little shy, but yes, the whole place is talking about the girl who's buying out our nursery." Dee Dee giggled. "I was wondering how long it was going to take you to come see my room."

"Your room! What is this room?"

"This is the room where I create new flowers!" said Dee Dee excitedly. "Would you like to create one yourself?"

"Of course I would."

"Well, then come on in." Dee Dee, grabbed my hand and pulled me into the room.

Glitz followed, stopping shyly by the doorway, "Murranda, can I come in and help you make a flower or even just watch you?"

"Sure you can. I could use the help."

Inside the flower room, the only source of light came in the form of miniature fireflies and a single stream of light from the ceiling in the center of the room.

The center light pointed down to what appeared to be a cast iron pot with liquid and smoke billowing over the edges. I could also see tall shelves around the pot filled with jars, boxes and containers. Some looked like jars of paint with different shades of color. The smaller containers looked like perfume bottles. I also saw boxes decorated with pictures of different flowers.

"So, how does this work, Dee Dee? What do I need to do?"

"Oh, it's easy," Dee Dee replied as Flutter nodded in agreement.

"The first thing you do is decide on what your flower is going to look like. Is it going to be a rose, or a daisy, or an orchid maybe? Then you decide on how your flower is going to smell and finally, you pick a color. Just take the box or jar from the shelf, open it, and pour a little into the pot. The pot will mix everything together and will show you what your flower looks like. Once you're finished, you grab one of the vials over there and fill it with your potion, then hand it to me. I'll take one of my seedlings and pour the potion on it. Once all of that is done, you will have your very own, one of a kind flower."

I listened in amazement.

"Next is the most important part of all. You will need to know how to take care of the flower."

"Oh don't worry. We know... I mean, she knows how to take care of flowers. You just have to give them sunlight and water," Glitz said raising his hand in the air.

"Well, there is more to it than just that Glitz," Dee Dee explained. "You have to give it drops of water depending on what day it is. For example, if it's the first day of the month then you ONLY give it 1 drop of water, and if it's the 2nd day of the month, you give it 2 drops of water, and so forth."

"Oh, I understand," I replied.

Glitz raised his hand again and Dee Dee pointed at him. "What if Murranda wants to make more than one flower, but she wants them both to be the same, does that mean she has to remember everything she did when she made the first one?"

Dee Dee laughed. "Well, in the past the answer to that question would have been YES. But, you see I have invented the multi-box."

"Multi-box?" Glitz asked.

"Yes. With the multi-box, I can put her seed in, then Murranda can tell me how many seeds she wants. I say the number she has given me out loud, shake the box that number of times and when I open the box, voila! She will find the correct number of seeds."

"Wow! That is neat." I exclaimed.

"So, are you ready to get started on your flower my dear?" Dee Dee asked as she put her hand behind my back and guided me to the spot.

"I sure am. " I replied.

"What do you want your flower to look like?" asked Dee Dee.

"Goodness, there's so much to choose from. I don't know where to start." I said looking at all the boxes and labels.

"Let's see, I remember my mother's last diary entry stated that her favorite flower was a rose. So, I will make mine a rose, in honor of her."

I picked up the box with the picture of a rose, opened it and poured what looked like pink chalk dust into the pot.

"What do I want my rose to smell like? I could just let it smell like a rose, but I think I want it to be more than just that."

I looked around at all the perfume bottles and read each label until I found one called garden paradise. I opened it to see what it smelled like—it was lovely! I added that to the pot but, I also wanted something more.

My favorite scent is the aroma created when our chef makes cookies and cakes. I wonder if I can find a similar scent.

Flutter must've heard me talking to myself. She flew up to the top shelf and glowed brightly so I would see the bottle she was next to. I reached up and grabbed it. It read "Cookies & Cakes."

"Well how about that! Just what I was looking for! Thanks Flutter," I said, patting her on the head with my finger.

"Dee Dee can I mix the scents together or is that bad?"

"Oh you can do anything you want. It's just that your flower will have a different scent each time you smell it."

I opened and poured both bottles into the pot. I could smell the fragrance of flowers and the yummy sweet smell of cakes and cookies. It made me smile.

Now to choose my colors. I want my flower to be able to change colors. I want it to be kind of iridescent. I reached up for the pink and light purple and poured those in, along with some sky blue and a pinch from the jar labeled color changer.

While I was busy creating my flowers, Glitz got excited and started handing me any and every jar he could get his hands on.

"Look at this jar Murranda. This one says SPARKLE and this one...this one says DANCE let's use these." Glitz said with glee.

He was running around like an excited little kid, grabbing this jar and that. Suddenly, he tripped over a box that hit one of the shelves, knocking two open jars into the pot.

One jar splattered all over my arm as well as into the pot. It was a smoky-black ink. The other jar was pure white—so white that the other colors I had put in all turned pure white.

"Oh no Glitz! What have you done to my flower colors?" I cried.

I quickly tried to readjust by adding more of the colors to see if I could get them back, but everything I added just turned as white as the purest snow, except for the center.

Right there, in the middle, I noticed a black shadowy figure moving around. When I took a closer look, I noticed that it was copying everything I did.

"Dee Dee, come see what's happening. I have tried to add colors back to this but it's still white. What do you think I can do?"

"Let's see what spilled into your pot," she said.

I grabbed the 2 jars and showed them to her. Glitz and Flutter, nervous about what would happen, hid behind some boxes in the corner.

"Oh I see what happened," Dee Dee said shaking her head. "Murranda did any of the black stuff get on you before it fell into the pot?"

"Yes it did. Why?" I asked.

"It's called SHADOW and if some of it got on you as well as in the pot, the black moving figure you see is your shadow. It's also a shadow of anyone that you come in contact with. As you can see, there is your shadow and because I am next to you, my shadow appears also, but a little lighter than yours. Anything you do will appear in the shadow, just as if you were outside."

"But what about the white stuff that is not letting me add color to my rose?" I asked with a tear in my eye.

"Well," she said. "That one is called SNOW WHITE. It's kind of like bleach—it removes every color except Shadow. Permanently. You see, with the inky mixture getting on you and the pot, you have become one with your flower. So, no matter how far away you are from the rose it can still show what you are doing and who you are with."

I walked closer to the pot to get a better look. I waved my arms and the shadow waved too. That got me thinking.

"Wait a minute," I said, "if this flower will show a shadow of what I am doing and who I meet and sort of where I am, then my father, or anyone else I give the flower to, can see this and will not have to worry as much about me."

"That is true," Dee Dee said as she nodded.

Glitz slinked out of the corner crying, "I'm sorry, I'm sorry. I am so very sorry Murranda. We can start all over and make you another one, a better one, and I won't do anything wrong this time. Don't be mad at me, please."

I leaned over the pot and took a sniff. It still smelled like flowers, cookies and cake. I looked down at Glitz groveling at my feet.

"Oh Glitz, you didn't do anything wrong. In fact, you made it better than I could have ever dreamed."

"I did?" he asked, wiping the tears from his eyes. "How is that possible? You had all those pretty colors in there and now they're all gone. All you have left is this white and black rose. How did I make it better?"

"Don't you see, Glitz. With the rose as it is now, I can go on my journey and my father will not have to worry about me. He can see everything I'm doing and everywhere I'm going."

"Journey?" Glitz and Dee Dee shouted. "What journey?"

"Oh, that's right, I haven't told you guys the whole story. Once I help my father with the garden, I am going on a journey to find something that I must have."

"WOW! That sounds exciting. What are you looking for?" asked Dee Dee.

"That is the strange part," I said, "I don't know what I'm looking for, but something inside me is telling me that I must look for it."

They looked at each other then back at me and shrugged their shoulders and nodded their heads.

"Now that I have this amazing rose, my father, and anyone else I give a seed to, will be able to see me on my journey and know that I am alright. It will be like they're on the journey with me."

Dee Dee reached down and grabbed a vial sitting alongside the pot. "So this means you want to keep the rose as it is, shadow and all?"

"Oh yes, just like it is," I said, with a huge grin. "In fact, I want a dozen of them to take with me. This way if I need to ask for shelter at a nice village or town, I can offer them a flower or create a garden for them as a thank you. Then they can watch me as I continue on my journey."

Dee Dee filled the vial with the rose potion, "There is just one more thing you need to do now Murranda. You must name your flower."

"Yea! Murranda what are you going to name it?" Glitz asked excitedly.

As I thought about a perfect name for my rose I watched Flutter fly to where the seedlings were. They were almost as big as she was. She managed to grab them and I watched as she flew it over to Dee Dee to fill. I heard Glitz say, "Well, Murry, I mean Murranda what are you going to call it?"

"Glitz, what did you just call me?" I asked.

"I called you Murranda. Why?" He replied.

"No, no, before that? You called me something else. Murry! That's it. I will call it THE MURRY ROSE" I said with a gleam in my eye.

Everyone smiled while Dee Dee took the filled seedling and put it in the Multi Box. She said the number twelve and shook it twelve times. She opened the box and poured twelve seeds into my hand.

"There you go Murranda. Twelve Murry Rose seeds."

I was so happy that I gave one of them to Dee Dee. "I want you to have one of my seeds so you and Flutter can follow me on my journey. That's my way of saying thank you for all your help in letting me create this perfect gift for my father."

"Thank you, Murranda," said Dee Dee as she and Flutter hugged me.

I was happy and at peace knowing that once I returned to my father we would start working on the garden and plant one of my Murry Roses. It would grow, and my father would be able to watch me, his "Little Sunshine," head off on my own adventure. He would be able to find comfort in knowing what I was doing and where I was at all times.

CHAPTER 2

We left the flower room and headed to the counter to pay for my purchases. Along the way we picked up some gardening supplies and plant food. "Don't forget what I told you about taking care of your Murry Rose," Dee Dee reminded me.

"I won't. But I can take care of the other flowers the normal way. Correct?"

Dee Dee nodded.

"It's best to water them from the side and not directly on top," explained one of the elves helping me at the counter. Another elf totaled everything while others bagged my purchases.

Just then, I had a strange feeling that I was being watched or stared at.

I looked around and all I could see were other people shopping. A few humans, a couple of centaurs, a gnome, and a sprite, but they were all busy.

I looked toward the front window and that was when I first saw the unicorn. It was standing behind a berry bush, but staring directly at me.

I felt as if I had seen it before. Maybe in a dream or one of the stories I had read. The unicorn was so beautiful. Its body was a spectacular iridescent color. Depending on the light I could see some light pink, blue, green, and purple. The same colors were also on its mane and tail. Its horn was so shiny, it was nearly blinding.

This creature was so beautiful that it didn't look real. In fact, it looked somewhat like one of the unicorn figurines my mother collected. I leaned over to Glitz to ask if he had ever seen anything so lovely, but when I pointed to where it was... the unicorn vanished.

"I don't see anything Murry." Glitz said looking outside.

I was confused, but shrugged it off to my imagination.

"Oh well, I guess it was nothing," I said grabbing a few bags and heading back to the carriage.

While I was getting my things loaded and thanking Dee Dee, Flutter and everyone else for all their help, I looked around for Glitz. I really wanted to thank him for helping me.

Instead Glitz ran towards me waving his arms and yelling, "Don't leave, don't leave, Murranda. Wait for me. I want to come with you on your journey. Please, don't leave."

"You want to what?" I asked.

"Please Murry, let me come with you. I can keep you company, and tell you the best places to go and where not to go." Glitz said. "You really shouldn't be traveling alone on your journey. It could be dangerous."

"Now you sound like my father."

"Well, your father is right. I know everything about Xeenoephillia. I know you're not sure where you're going or what you're looking for, but I can lead you to exciting places full of adventure and beauty. Oh! Please Murranda let me come with you!"

Maybe he was right. Maybe having a guide would be helpful and having company wouldn't be at all bad. "Okay Glitz, you can join me," I said, helping him into the carriage.

"Thanks Murry. Could we stop by my place so I can pick up a few things?"

I nodded.

On our way to Glitz's home we stopped to pick up some other things we would need. We stopped by a bookshop, where I bought some journals for recording my stories and adventures; an art and music store to pick up sketchpads and other art supplies plus extra guitar strings for my guitar.

"You play the guitar?" asked Glitz. "That's great. I play the fairy flute. Maybe on our journey we can play together."

"That would be nice," I said. "Now where do you live Glitz?"

"Oh you turn there," he said, pointing towards the edge of the forest. "Just there, into the small rain forest and I am just inside, not far."

"You live in the rain forest?" I blurted out.

He couldn't help but laugh at my question. "Oh Murry! You forget. I am a fairy. We don't live in houses. We live with nature, just like the birds and the squirrels. I live inside an old tree stump." He pointed out an old oak tree stump that looked like it had a door and tiny windows carved into it.

"Wow! I have always wanted to see where fairies live." I exclaimed. I looked around and saw there were several fairy homes and many tiny fairies flying about.

"I will be right back," said Glitz. Then he shrunk himself back down to fairy size and flew into his stump.

While I waited for him to gather his things and return, I took a moment to look around. I couldn't believe what I was seeing. The fairies were flying in and out of their little homes—some in flowers, others in trees. There were even some gathered around the small waterfall caves. I saw Glitz flying back my way.

He was flying so fast, he spooked the horses. They reared up and bolted off.

"Whoa! Stop Lightning! Stop Steel Blade!" I cried.

I grabbed the reins and pulled back, but I could barely control them.

Suddenly two tiny fairies zipped past my head. I opened my mouth to yell for them to be careful, but they flew straight to the horses' ears and spoke to them.

The next thing I knew, the horses slowed down to a stop.

"Wow! Thank you!" I said, breathless. I reached back to make sure everything in the carriage was alright, then I looked around for Glitz but he was nowhere in sight.

Finally, I saw something moving behind one of the boxes. I moved it to the side and asked, "Glitz is that you? It might help if you made yourself larger."

He made himself human size and we made our way back to my house. I knew my father would be worried by now. We'd taken longer than I had expected.

Just as I thought, when we approached the house, there was my father standing at the front door, waiting.

"What took you so long Sunshine? I was getting worried," he said, helping me off the buggy.

"What did you get?" he asked eying the bags. "Good gracious child, did you leave anything for other people to buy?"

Glitz made his way down and politely bowed to my father.

"Who is this?"

"Hi, I'm Glitz. I am a fairy and Murry's friend. She said I could join her on her adventure."

"Oh really?" Father said, stroking his goatee. "I do see the wings, but you look too big to be a fairy."

"Well sir, we fairies can grow to this size so you mortals can see us better."

"Yes Father. Glitz is going to join me so I will have some company."

I patted him on the back and grabbed some things out of the buggy. "He knows a lot about Xeenoephillia. He knows things I should see and also, places I should avoid."

"I can keep Murry from becoming lost on the journey, sir." Glitz said following me into the garden carrying a box of flowers.

"Get lost? You don't even know where you're going." Father said, shaking his head and grabbing the last of the boxes.

"Now Father, please don't start. We have lots to do and I don't want us to argue. I'll be fine. I promise."

I gathered the flowers and began planning how I was going to arrange them for my mother's birthday garden.

Father, Glitz and I arranged seeds in areas where we felt the flowers should be planted. I recalled reading in one of my mother's diaries about a labyrinth. She would walk through it and dream of having a garden arranged in that way. The decision was made! We had to plant a labyrinth garden.

LABYRINTH

During my childhood, Father would tell stories explaining the labyrinth and its special meaning for our family. I knew if we made her a labyrinth garden, Mother would be so happy that her spirit might come down and walk through it. Father agreed that it was a wonderful idea.

While I was getting everything we needed for the garden, Father patterned out the labyrinth in the dirt with the rake. Now all we had to do was plant the flower seeds in the right places.

While we worked, Glitz began telling Father of all the different places and things we might encounter on our journey. He warned of places, people, and things we should avoid, especially the place known as the Shadow Land.

In the Shadow Land there was a lot of dark magic and evil creatures dwelled. Glitz's tales did not sit well with my father, but I assured him that I did not have any desire to visit that place. Father's eyes rose when he heard voices coming from the talking flowers.

"When is she going to give him his flower, The Murry Rose," they whispered.

"Wait! We have talking flowers here now!" Father asked, walking toward them.

He knelt down to get a closer look. "So what is this Murry Rose and more importantly, how can you be talking?"

"As we told your daughter, if we did not talk how would you know what we wanted or needed," said one of the flowers with a smirk.

"Oh, I see you've met the chatty callies. That's what I named them because they cannot stop talking and they look like calla lilies," I said. "I was going to wait and show you my surprise flower after we finished everything else. But someone couldn't keep its petals shut." I turned my head toward the chatting calla lilies. One of them closed its petals as if to hide from me.

"You see Father, there was a room in the flower nursery called 'Make your own flower!' In this room you could make your very own one of a kind flower. So I made one especially for you."

"And I helped!" Glitz added with a big smile as he showed Father the seeds.

"One of a kind, huh? Then why do I see eleven seeds?" Father asked.

"Well okay! Maybe eleven of a kind," I said. Everyone laughed.

"So, what is so special about this flower other than it came from you, Sunshine."

"Well, Father, when it blooms into a rose, it will be pure white. You might say it will be as white as a snowfall at Christmastime, except for the center of the rose. In the center you will see a shadow. The shadow will be of me. It will allow you to see me wherever I am and whomever I'm with during my journey. In a way Father, it would be as though you were with me just by watching the shadow in the rose. There is also one more thing. This special rose will smell like my two favorite things."

"Flowers and desserts," he said laughing with a tear in his eye.

"Oh Murry, you made your daddy cry," said Glitz searching for a tissue.

I leaned my head on Father's chest. "Don't cry Father. It's okay if you don't like your gift."

"Like it? I love it, Sunshine." Then he kissed my forehead.

"Where should we plant this one Murry?" Glitz asked.

Father and I looked around the labyrinth garden. We then looked at each other and smiled. We both knew what the other was thinking. Father went into the work shed and came back with golden rocks. He walked to the center of the labyrinth and made a circle with the rocks.

"That is perfect, Father! We will plant it there."

Father dug a small hole, and I dropped in one seed, and then covered it with the soil.

Father was about to water the plant until Glitz yelled, "NO! WAIT! NOT like that! You will kill it."

"Glitz is right Father. There is a special way to take care of this flower."

I took a water dropper from my pocket. "You can give it a drop of water depending on the day of the month. I explained, repeating Dee Dee's instructions

"I see."

"Today is the 5th day of the month. So, that must mean we give this little one five drops to start its new life." With that, Father, Glitz, and I together held the water dropper and gave it five drops of water.

We were finally finished planting my mother's birthday garden. As the sun set over the lake, I smelled a delicious aroma coming from the house.

"Come Glitz, let's get ready for dinner. It's getting late and I am hungry. Plus we have to get to bed early tonight so we can have an early start in the morning."

I took Glitz by the hand and led him into the house to show him where he would sleep.

While we cleaned up for dinner, I could not stop thinking about the unicorn I saw outside the flower store. I had such a strong feeling that I had seen it before. I sat by the window brushing my hair and looking out onto the lake and fields, wondering if maybe, just maybe, the unicorn followed us here.

"Sunshine! Glitz! It's time for dinner." Father called from downstairs.

Glitz and I headed down the hallway to the spiral staircase. He stopped and noticed the picture of Mother and Father on the wall.

"Is that your mother?" he asked, pointing to the picture.

"Yes that's her."

"Wow! She's was so beautiful," he said. Glitz looked at the picture and then looked at me. "You look a lot like her."

"Thank you," I replied. "Let's go down to dinner. I'll show you the rest of the house later. Last one down is a rotten egg!"

We raced down the stairs and into the dining room. There in front of us was a long table filled with all types of goodies and treats.

"Wow! This is enough for a banquet, and there are only three or us. What are we going to do with the rest of the food?" asked Glitz.

"I thought you could take it with you on your trip. I'll have the cook pack it for you."

"Thank you Father. That's a great idea."

Jeffery walked over to Glitz. He knelt down and said, "I've been doing some reading on fairies. I think I might have gotten your dinner just right. If I'm not mistaken, fairies' favorite drink is honeysuckle juice, correct?"

"Wow! You've got some honeysuckle juice!" exclaimed Glitz jumping up and down in his chair.

I looked over at Father and said, "Jeffrey, you must have spent hours milking the honeysuckles."

Father laughed. "We also have boysenberry pie for dessert and carrots, spinach, and rutabagas."

"You all are the best," said Glitz. "I haven't eaten this good in years."

Father and I had roasted duck with broccoli and spinach in a cream sauce with baby onions. We had fresh rolls and, one of my favorites, a cheesecake for dessert.

"Thank you Jeffrey. Tell the cook she did an excellent job."

"Will do young madam. Is there anything else I can do for you?"

"No, we're good for now, Jeffrey," said Father. I noticed him looking outside at the garden as Jeffery walked away. I kept eating my dinner and talking with Glitz about all the things we were going to do on our journey. Then, Glitz and I looked up and saw that Father had a tear in his eye.

"What's wrong Father? Now you look like you've got the world on your shoulders."

He gave a big sigh and looked at Glitz and I. "I cannot help but ask why you have to go now. The garden isn't even in bloom. The plant with the special rose has not even come up to show itself. Can I truly let you go without even knowing how you're going to be?"

I put down my fork and looked at Father. "We'll be okay. Glitz knows the area and he will not let any harm come to me."

"Yes, she is right sir. I won't let any harm come to her." Glitz said wrapping his small arms on my shoulders.

"A fairy as your personal bodyguard? I still think you should take someone bigger and stronger with you. No offense, Glitz."

He walked over to me putting one hand on my shoulder and the other on Glitz. "I am sure you have your own special skills, but this is my only daughter, so I have a right to worry. We have many young men who could accompany you on your journey."

I stood and said, "We've already discussed this. I'm going alone; well with Glitz and no one else."

"But Sunshine," Father said, "without the rose that has your shadow, how will I know where you are and how you're doing? How can I let you go now? Please, let's discuss this. Is there any good reason why you and Glitz cannot wait until the garden has bloomed and the Murry rose has opened to show its shadow? Can you please wait until then? I beg of you! That way I can be on your journey with you and I won't worry; at least not as much. PLEASE Sunshine. Look at this from my point of view."

"I think he's makes a good point," said Glitz.

As eager as I was to go, I agreed to Father's terms. I told Father that once the rose plant had grown, I would leave immediately; no questions asked and no other restrictions.

He nodded in agreement and gave me a big hug. Even though I couldn't leave right away, I understood where my father was coming from. There had only been the two of us since my mother was gone. We were so very close that the whole idea of me leaving was tearing him apart.

"Well, Glitz, it's getting late, and I'm tired. What about you?"

"I'm not tired at all," he said, yawning.

"Come on! Let's go upstairs. We can at least talk until we fall asleep. I'll show you around the house first."

"Okay," he said.

We rose from the table, and I walked over to give Father a kiss. "Goodnight, Father. Now remember, you said as soon as the flower has bloomed I can leave."

"I'll remember. Goodnight Sunshine. Goodnight Glitz. I have to say, if anyone is to go with my daughter, I'm glad it's you."

We headed up the stairs. Glitz looked around at the artwork on the ceilings. He looked at the fine china in the cabinets and all the different unicorns. "I see you really like unicorns"

"Mother collected them before I was born, and they were passed on to me. Dad said she had a fascination with them. I think a part of her wished she could be a unicorn, an immortal creature of peace and goodness."

It was late when I finished showing Glitz the rest of the house, so we went into my room and got ready for bed.

I lay in bed for awhile, thinking about the trip. It was very quiet. Everyone else was fast asleep. Suddenly, I heard a rustling sound coming from the woods and garden just outside my window.

I stood up and looked outside. It was the unicorn—the same one I had seen earlier.

The unicorn walked across the path and into the labyrinth, stopping periodically to nod her head down and point.

At each spot she lowered her head and with the tip of her horn she touched a flower. As if by magic, it would grow.

She would touch one spot, and roses would appear, another spot produced daisies while another spot became orchids. Then she turned and touched other spots and flowers grew that danced and changed colors. She would speak to the flowers and tell them to wake up.

When she approached the calla lilies, one started to scream "IT'S YOU! IT'S YOU!"

"Shhh!" said another, "the humans are asleep, stupid." Looking at the unicorn, it asked, "What are you doing here?"

The unicorn did not answer. She went about her business, touching flowers along the garden, until she got to the center of the labyrinth and the Murry Rose.

She once again lowered her head and with the tip of her horn pointed at the Murry Rose and said, "Wake up little one. We must help Murranda. Her father wants her to wait until the garden has grown. I think we should give it a little help and let her journey begin. So wake up. Show your beautiful self to the world."

The Murry rose grew from the ground a little at a time. It bloomed slowly and finally opened, with its white petals growing bigger and bigger. The stem grew longer and longer until it became a beautiful white rose with a black center.

The unicorn looked around at her work. She saw the beautiful flowers standing there dancing and playing melodies, while some sparkled and glittered.

As she admired the Murry rose, a little tear came into her eye.

The sun started to rise, and she realized it was time for her to leave. She pranced out of the labyrinth, into the woods and disappeared.

When the sun came up the next morning, I woke up and yawned. *What a lovely dream, I had.* I looked over to where Glitz had slept, but he wasn't there.

"Glitz, where are you?" I called.

"Up here," he replied, from above me. "I'm on the top shelf sitting on a unicorn figurine. I woke early and didn't want to disturb you. You were sleeping so peacefully, so I started looking at your unicorn collection. This one is beautiful. The color is so see-thru and shiny."

"Yes, that's called an iridescent. The color changes depending on how the light hits it," I explained.

"The light made this one look like a rainbow."

"Yes, I call that my Rainbow Unicorn. Father says it was Mom's favorite, so I keep it in a special spot. Please be careful."

"Oh, I won't break it," said Glitz.

"Well, I guess we should get ready for breakfast," I said, getting out of bed.

I went to the bathroom to brush my teeth and hair. Before I could get settled, there was a knock on the door.

"Come in."

Jeffrey came into the room.

"Young madam, there's something outside you need to see."

"What is it? Is it Father?"

"No," he said, "but you need to come. It's your garden."

I was terribly worried that something bad had happened. "What happened? Did someone get in there and destroy it?"

I dropped the brush and ran out into the hallway, down the stairs and into the garden. When I saw it, I couldn't believe my eyes.

The flowers had all blossomed; the roses, the daisies and daffodils, the ones that sparkled and danced, the ones that glittered, and the ones that played fireworks and music. Then I noticed the center plant. Could it be? Was it really my flower, the Murry Rose? Had it truly bloomed? I walked over to it. As I got closer, I looked into the center and saw my shadow.

"It's my rose!" I said. "Oh Glitz, Glitz, take a look."

Glitz flew down the stairs. "Wow, Murray! I did not do this."

"Do what? I know you didn't do it. You were with me," I said, looking at my rose.

"The only ones who have the power to make flowers grow this fast are fairies and unicorns. Did any of your figurines come to life?" he asked scratching his little head.

I laughed. "No, I don't think so. Do you know of any other fairies around who could have done this? Maybe one of them heard my dream-wish that the garden would grow faster. Or could it have been the unicorn I saw at the flower store? No, it couldn't have been. It wouldn't have followed us all the way over here. Or would it?"

As Glitz and I looked on in amazement, Father came down the stairs.

"What's all the racket? Why is everyone talking about the garden? What's going on?"

He looked out and couldn't believe his eyes. "It can't be. It can't be," he said, over and over.

"Father it's true. The garden has grown. And look," I said pointing. "It's my Murry Rose; with the shadow of me and all of us. Now, Father, I can start on my journey!" I exclaimed, jumping into his arms.

Father couldn't believe it. But he knew it was true. With a sad look in his eyes, he looked into mine.

"A promise is a promise, and I did say once the garden had bloomed and the flower had come to life, I would let you go." He squeezed my hand.

"This is the hardest thing I've ever had to do, Sunshine since your mother died. You must promise to come back to me and be safe and find ways of contacting me if you need anything at all."

"Father, I promise. Oh Glitz, let's gets ready. We have lots to do and a lot of ground to cover."

I ran upstairs. Jeffery prepared breakfast for both of us and brought it to my room so we could eat as we packed.

I couldn't believe it. The flowers have bloomed!

Everything was going great and I now could go on my journey and find the "thing" I needed, even though I still didn't know what it was. That's the strange part. But, I know somewhere; somehow I'll find it.

I packed my bags with plenty of clothes and made sure to pack my mother's guitar and my artwork. I handed a couple of bags to the servants to take to the buggy.

Glitz was already downstairs. Fairies don't have a lot to pack. He made sure everything was in its proper place. Knowing him, he was also making sure they had plenty of honeysuckle juice and boysenberry pie. I looked around and grabbed my mother's picture.

"Mother," I said, speaking to the picture, "I can't believe I'm finally going on my journey. I wish you were here. I wish I knew what I was looking for. Having your picture with me will be almost like having you there with me."

I grabbed a smaller copy of Mother and Father's wedding photo and put it in my bag. As I went down with my last bag in hand, I saw my father in the garden sitting beside the Murry Rose, looking very somber. I gave my last bag to the servant to place in the carriage, and walked over to Father.

I knelt down by his feet and put my head on his lap. "Father, you knew this day would come; the day when I would have to leave.

"I know, Sunshine. My only problem is that I thought it would be with a young man in your arms, where you would be changing your last name and getting married. I could handle that more than you going on this journey into the unknown; not knowing where you're going or what you're looking for, yet so intent on finding something. That's what scares me. At least, as you said, I'll have this flower that will trace your journey and hopefully it will make me feel that I'm with you. Always know in your heart that if you ever need me, just find a way of contacting me. I'll find you through your rose."

We stood and gave each other a great big hug. It was the warmest and saddest hug I'd ever had. Father walked me to the carriage and helped me up. I looked at everyone and leaned over and gave Jeffrey a hug. He'd been part of the family for years.

"Jeffrey, please don't forget to feed the ducks and swans."

"I won't madam."

"And don't forget to keep watch on the rose and follow my journey."

"You have no worry there young madam. I will always be sure and watch how you're doing. Well, Glitz, my new friend, here's all your supplies. I got you 5 bottles of honeysuckle juice, some boysenberry pie and everything else you will need."

"Thank you sir."

" Call me Jeffrey. Since you're with Murranda you're part of the family now."

"Well thank you all. I promise I'll keep Murry safe. I'll make sure she stays on the right path and away from the Shadow Land."

"Well Glitz, are you ready?" I asked, grabbing the reins to the horses.

"Yep! Let's go."

I steered the horses toward the gates, looked back and waved good-bye, not knowing when I'd be back to see them again, but I knew in my heart that this journey would be a journey I'd never forget.

3

CHAPTER 3

We were finally on our way! I was excited and a little scared. I didn't know what to expect. I didn't even know where we were going or what I was looking for.

I told myself that a person had to be a fool to go on this type of adventure but, deep down I knew it was something I had to do.

Once we had travelled past the edge of my home, Glitz played his fairy flute, while I hummed along. While we played and laughed, Glitz explained some of things we might encounter along the way.

He told me tales of the elves, giants, and trolls. He said we might come across pirates, and if we were lucky, we might even see a mermaid. There was also the chance we would meet a unicorn or two.

I had a strange feeling that my unicorn friend was following me; that is, if it was my friend—though I had no reason to think otherwise.

Glitz again warned me of the Shadow Land and all of its different creatures—werewolves, vampires, witches and other dangerous things. He also told me about the evil Sorceress and the Dark Prince who ruled over the Shadow Land. There were also Shadow people who protected the land, as well as talking trees.

We rode for hours, taking in the sights and stopping along the way to rest the horses and sit for a while to eat. During one of the stops, Glitz told me a story about a man who, because of his greed, was changed into an owl; not just an ordinary owl, a golden owl.

He heard this story from other fairies, who heard it from elves who had heard it from the leprechauns. The owl, they say, was a man who was a tax collector. He became very rich, but in turn was consumed by his greed. The sorceress cast a spell on him and turned him into a golden owl. He had the ability to fly but when his feathers would molt or when people would pull on them, the gold turned as heavy as bricks.

It was getting late, so we decided to set up camp for the night. I was still so excited I couldn't sleep. All I could do was write in my journal by the campfire and draw pictures of what had happened so far. I drew pictures of my father, the house, and the garden labyrinth and of course of the Murry Rose.

I felt that Father was sitting by the rose watching to see how I was doing. He would know that at the moment I was safe.

As we lay by the campfire, Glitz formed himself as tiny as a fairy and lay between some leaves. I took the blanket Jeffrey packed and a pillow my mother had made, and settled in by the campfire. I couldn't help but wonder what we would encounter, who we would meet and what it was we needed to look for. I had no idea, but it was something I needed to do.

"So, Murranda," Glitz said, "do you think you will ever figure out what you're looking for?"

"I'm not sure. I hope so. Just experiencing this adventure is kind of exciting in itself. As my father said, I've never been out on my own. I feel close to Mother like this. She loved to go on adventures with Father before I was born. I wonder if she would be proud of me following in her footsteps?"

I looked over at Glitz as I was talking and saw that he had fallen asleep.

I put out the fire, snuggled into my blanket, curled up and finally fell asleep. I dreamed of the adventures we would have. Mother and Father were with me in my dreams, as well as the unicorn. It was as though everywhere I went, I could see it—behind a tree, or a bush, coming around the corner of a building. *Was this unicorn coming after me? Was it curious? Why was it following me? Why was it always in my dreams?*

The next morning we woke up, gathered our belongings, got back in the buggy and headed out. Soon, we came across a small dirt road. We left the main road and decided to take it.

There were other carriages on this road with families aboard. Looking at their faces, they all seemed excited. In fact, there were a lot of people on this road. Glitz and I wondered what was going on, so we stopped one of the buggies and asked.

"Excuse me, there seems to be a lot of people going this way. Is there some danger ahead?" I asked a couple.

"Oh, there's no danger," replied the woman. "We're actually going to a gypsy fair just over the hill. You should come along. They have it every year. Follow us. We'll show you."

Glitz and I looked at each other, "Did she say Gypsy Fair?" he asked.

"Yeah, is there something wrong with that?"

"You need to be careful with gypsies. They can be tricky. They're known to be thieves. So we shouldn't take a lot of valuables with us when we stop, and we should put a cover over the carriage to avoid unwanted trouble."

"Okay," I said. "I've heard about gypsies. But don't worry so much," I said nudging him playfully.

"Come on Glitz this should be fun. We've been riding for a while, we should enjoy some fun time. We're really not in a time frame. Besides, this is supposed to be an adventure."

"Sure! Why not? This will be a great story."

We followed the young couple. There were many travelers with them. Some were on horseback, others on unique creatures that were equal parts lion and eagle. The elves flew around on them. There was even an Indian on a horse as well as an ogre and a giant following behind him.

Every creature seemed to be smiling and friendly enough—except the ogre of course. They didn't appear to be hungry, so I didn't believe we were in danger of being eaten.

We came over a small hill and arrived at the fair—and what a fair it was!

There were giant tents with bright colors and lots of people around wearing colorful outfits and an assortment of dangling jewelry.

Some of the performers were on tall stilts that made them look like skinny giants. Some were on huge balls rolling around. Others were contortionists; turning their bodies inside out and making themselves look like human wheels rolling around.

We saw fire-eaters, snake charmers and fortune-tellers. Some people were selling clothes and jewelry. Others were selling little toys for the kids. There were also some carts with food and drinks. It all looked like fun.

On the other side, there were people blowing out fire with fire sticks. We even saw belly dancers and musicians.

"Wow, good thing I've got my guitar," I declared. "Maybe I can join in with them."

"Be careful," said Glitz. "A lot of gypsies are not very friendly unless they're with other gypsies. They pretend to be friendly just so they can collect some money. Other than that, they usually stick with their own kind."

"Oh, I'm sure we can make some friends," I said with confidence.

As we walked around, I had the feeling that someone was staring at me. Everywhere I looked I thought I was seeing the unicorn. Around a corner, by the tent, sometimes behind people, see it.

While I was looking around, a woman approached me. She was middle aged, very pretty with dark brown hair and eyes. She wore a colorful outfit with a lot of gold bracelets, necklaces and earrings.

As she came nearer, she had a strange look in her eyes. I wondered if something was wrong. Was she looking past me at someone else? I turned and looked around.

"Can I help you?" I asked.

"Well," she said, "maybe I can help you."

"What do you mean you can help me?"

"No need for fear child. I'm a fortune teller. My name is Phoebe," she waved her hand to me. "Come. You and I need to talk."

"Be careful!" said Glitz. "Remember what I said. Gypsies can be very tricky."

"I'll be fine Glitz," I said, patting him on the back, "I want to hear what this woman has to say."

"Your friend is right. We are tricky. Normally, I sell jewelry and silk. I truly mean you no harm but, I know something. Something about your journey. There are some things you need to know."

I was taken aback by her mention of the journey. I looked at Glitz and he shrugged his shoulders.

"How do you know?"

"I know many things. Come, let us talk more."

"Okay." I said.

We followed her to one of the smaller tents. Once inside she turned to me and began to speak.

"Here is what I know. You're going to come across some interesting characters and people during your travels. Some you will be able to tell are safe. You must invite them with you on your journey for they have a purpose in where you're going. There are some you will encounter who will need your help before you can continue. There are also some people you need to be wary of. These people mean you harm and will cause danger throughout your journey. They will act as if they are your friends and can help you. Do not to fall for their treachery. I know you will be going to the Shadow Land, so I warn you to be careful of the dark castle."

"Whoa!" I cried out. "Wait just a minute; the Shadow Land? I would never go there. I know about that place and the dangers it holds."

"I know you are aware of the Shadow Land, but there will be a time in your journey when you will have to go there. You must be brave and beware of the dark castle. There are some things in there you will need in order to continue your journey, but there is evil lurking in there, also. You must beware of the dark prince and the sorceress."

Glitz was frightened. He did not want me to go to the Shadow Land, and I didn't blame him. I had no intention of going there no matter what Phoebe said.

"You will have two guides," she continued. "One is following you now and another is somewhere around but only appear during times of extreme danger. They will become an important part of your life."

"I am one of her guides." Glitz said. He took a step toward Phoebe. "I have been showing her where to go."

"I see you have," Phoebe smiled, "but there are two others unseen to you."

"Phoebe, can you answer one question for me?" I asked.

"I'll try. What is it?"

"Just what am I looking for? If you're all knowing please tell me, because I have no idea. I just know that whatever it is, I have to find it."

All Phoebe would say was, "Unfortunately, I cannot tell you that."

"You can't or won't tell me?" I asked. "Which is it?"

"I'm not allowed to tell you. The spirits are telling me that it is something you need to figure out on your own, but it is of great significance that you find it. You're doing the right thing by going on this journey, Murranda, and I do know you and I will meet again. Our paths will cross. When? I'm not sure." She turned around and motioned for us to follow.

"Now, be careful, young traveler. But before you leave, enjoy the fair. There are lots of things to see and tons to do. Stay as long as you need. You may find some things that will help you on your trip. Speaking of things you may need, why don't you come over here. I have a few things to show you."

I still wasn't sure I could trust her. But, my curiosity got the better of me, and I followed her anyway. She led me into what looked like a carriage dressed up to look like a cottage. It had curtains and a tent attached to make it broader. She told us to wait while she went inside.

We looked around to see what was going on. I could smell the aroma of all the food, and I was getting a little hungry. When she came out she was carrying some jewelry and a small box. There was a necklace with a black onyx and a ruby in the center.

She said, "You will need this necklace. Please wear it and try never to take it off. It will protect you through your journey."

Then she held out the box and said, "You will need this, too. You will know what it's for later." She opened the box and inside there was a beautiful ruby and black onyx ring.

She placed the necklace around my neck. I felt a calm come over me. Then I put the ring on too. It kind of tickled at first. I thought it felt weird so I took them off. The moment I did, something came over me. I felt worried and unsure of myself. I didn't feel safe. So I quickly put the necklace and ring back on. It was as though they were made for me; as if we were one.

"Thank you," I said. "What is this ring for?"

"You will know soon enough. Promise me you'll always wear it. It will guide you on your journey and so will the necklace."

"What are those other things you're holding?" I asked.

"I came across this bracelet and these earrings and thought they matched, so I'm hoping you will buy them. You know a girl's got to make a living," Phoebe said with a little giggle.

I looked at them. She was right. They did match. They were made of black onyx as well as rubies. I handed her a few coins.

She also had a gift for Glitz. It was a bag of stones. She said they too would help him on the journey. He would know what they were for later.

She handed Glitz a small vial attached to a necklace. She told him to wear it and keep it safe. He was to use it only when he knew it was an absolute must. It had the power to do many things, such as restore healing.

"You will know what to use this for when the right time comes. All you need is one drop into the mouth or on the spot where it's needed."

Glitz was curious as to what this was all about, but he just shook his head and said, "Thank you!"

We left Phoebe's tent and went out to take in the fair. I was enjoying the day, walking around seeing the sights and performances and eating the wonderful food. Glitz got tired of walking and was not feeling comfortable with the crowd, so he decided to shrink down to his fairy size and flutter around. There were other fairies flying about, perhaps he would find some he knew.

Suddenly that strange feeling returned. I still felt I was being followed, but I didn't know if it was Phoebe or someone else.

As the sun began to set, we realized how late it was getting, so we went back to our wagon. When we approached, there were people jumping on and off of it. The gypsies were ransacking our things.

I ran as fast as I could.

"That's our wagon! That's our wagon!" I yelled.

"Please! That's our stuff. We must have it."

Glitz flew as fast as he could to try to stop them but he was no match. The gypsies drove off with everything. All I could do was sit and cry.

Glitz flew back to me and then changed back into his child-like size.

"I'm sorry," he said, panting and breathless. "I tried to catch them."

"I know, Glitz. It's just that there were some things in there I needed. There was a bag with pictures of my mother, my sketch pads, my journal…"

"I know. There was a small bag of things I needed, too. I had a survival bag that fairies always carry and our food to last us through the journey."

"What are we going to do?" I thought sitting down along the edge of the grass.

Just then, I looked up and noticed a shiny object coming our way. As it got closer I could tell it had four legs and looked like a horse.

It was the unicorn; the same unicorn I saw at the flower shop. There was something wrapped around its horn. When it was close enough, I realized it was my bag of belongings. There was also a tiny bag on top that must have belonged to Glitz.

I ran to the unicorn and said, "Thank you! Thank you."

"You're welcome," replied the unicorn. "I'm sorry I couldn't stop the thieves and get your horse and wagon back. Are you okay?"

"Yes I am, thank you," I said. "My name is…"

"Murranda. I know. My name is Deena. I've known you for a very long time. I've watched you grow up since you were a child. I've been around your family for many years, and in my own way, I've taken care of you all."

"You've known my mother and father?" I asked.

"Yes, especially your mother."

"Wow, you look like some of the unicorn figurines she collected."

"Yes, Morinda was very well known and loved in our world."

"It's true. You do exist." I said in amazement.

"Some of the stories about us are true and some are myths. It's true, that only the pure of heart can see us as we really are. Others know us as horses," looking at Glitz she added, "unless they are mythical creatures such as fairies. Fairies can see us as we are."

Suddenly I heard Phoebe calling out to us. "I heard you yelling. Is everything alright?"

"We're okay Phoebe. We just had our wagon, horse and other things taken."

"I know I'm a gypsy, but I'll tell you one thing, some of these people can be just plain mean. Scavengers, the lot of them. Vagabonds survive on what we have and what we can take. As far as I'm concerned, we should survive on what we have or can earn. Things should be received as a gift not stolen. I'm so sorry about my people."

"It's okay. It's not just gypsies. There are bad people all over. They come in all shapes and sizes."

"Well, it's getting late, and you must be tired. Come. You can stay with me for the evening. Your horse will have to stay outside, though. We don't have room for her," Phoebe said with a strange look in her eye, as if she knew something she wasn't saying.

"Oh, she is not a horse…" Before I could say anything else Deena butted me as if to say hush.

Deena stayed with the other horses in a stall just behind Deena's tent. Glitz and I followed Phoebe back to the gypsy site. We were very thankful for her hospitality.

Before we went to sleep that evening, Glitz pulled me aside and said, "Murry, you forgot what Deena told you. Not all people can see them for what they really are. Only someone that is mystical, such as a fairy, or someone who is pure of heart can see."

"You're right Glitz I did forget. Thanks."

It was all so fascinating!

With all the excitement, I couldn't sleep, so I walked around outside to clear my head a bit. I was thinking about what I should do next. Where would be the best place to go in order to find what I needed?

I also thought about my father and what he was doing. What would he be thinking if he knew about our stolen cart? My mind was racing with so many things that I did not notice how far I had wandered from the tent. All of a sudden, I fell into a deep hole.

"Ouch!" I yelled.

I looked up and around and noticed the hole I had fallen into was quite deep. I grabbed at the sides to try to make my way out, but the walls it seemed were smooth and not easy to climb.

Then I heard a noise above me. It sounded as if it were coming out of some bushes.

"Help!" I cried "Somebody help me! I am down in this hole, and I've hurt my ankle. Please help me."

"Shhh! Be quiet," said a voice.

I was trying to see who had spoken when I noticed a cat peering into the hole.

"Hey there, little one. Be careful. You don't want to jump in here. This is not a safe place for you, or even me for that matter."

The little cat paced the edge of the hole, peering me. Suddenly he jumped in. He landed on his feet and looked around. He was a small, with grey and black markings kind of like a tiger. He had beautiful light brownish gold eyes and a couple of white markings. One of the spots was on the tip of his tail. And he also had a white star on his forehead.

"Well little one, I can see that you just don't listen now do you." I laughed. "I am glad you are here to keep me calm, but I don't know how you can help me."

"Are you ok?" asked the little cat. "Are you hurt?"

"It was you. You can talk?" I said, surprised.

"I think I twisted my ankle," I said, rubbing it. "I was trying to figure out how we can get out of here. This hole is so deep, and the walls are so slippery."

"Yea, I see that," said the cat. "You fell into a trap that was set for me and other animals like me."

"How can we get out of here?" I asked.

"One moment please," he said.

Just as I was wondering how he was going to get us out of this, he started to grow. As I watched, astonished, he grew bigger and bigger right before my eyes until he was about the size of a tiger.

At the same time, he was getting darker and darker; so dark, he was blending into the night sky. I did not know what to think or how to act. I was somewhat frightened of him.

"Don't be afraid," he said. "Jump on my back and hold on."

"What? "I asked.

"Trust me. Don't be afraid. I am a friend, and I'm here to get you out."

"What are you?" I asked.

"I will explain everything once we get you out of here. We have to go, before the trappers come back."

I jumped on his back, hanging on to him for dear life. He continued to get even bigger—almost as big as the hole itself. He grew so big, we were able to step out.

As soon as we were out of the hole, he carried me back towards the campsite. Once he felt we were safe, he shrank down to a less intimidating size.

"You can hop off now," he said.

"Thank you for getting me out of there," I said, dusting myself off.

"You are welcome. Now come follow me over here where it's safe."

He led me back to Phoebe's.

"My name Gray Sky, but you can call me Sky. That's what most around here call me."

"I'm Murranda," I replied. "But my friends call me Murry for short."

"Are you sure you are okay?" Sky asked, looking me over.

"Yes, I'm fine and thanks again."

By the time we got back to the tent, Sky had shrunk down to the size of an overgrown house cat. I saw Glitz flying toward me and then quickly grow to his boyish size.

"Where were you?" he yelled. "We have been looking everywhere for you."

"I heard a scream and woke up to see that you were not in the room with me, so I came out looking for you. Are you Ok?" He hugged me tightly.

"Yes, I'm fine Glitz. Nothing to worry about," I said trying to calm him down.

"This is Sky. He saved me from a hole I fell into."

Glitz looked at the small cat and said, "This cat saved you? How? "

"Well," I replied, "Sky is an interesting sort of cat."

"Yes, I am," Sky chimed in. "I am what is called a Chama Cat— part chameleon and part cat. I can blend into my surroundings like a chameleon, plus I can change my size as big or as small as I need."

Phoebe heard us talking and walked outside.

"Is everything okay? Did you find Murranda?"

"Yes we did," answered Glitz.

We all went inside. Deena came to the window of the tent carriage.

"Is everyone okay?" She asked, eyeing the cat. "Hi Sky."

"Hi Deena. Hi Phoebe. It has been a while since we crossed paths," Sky said. "How have you been?" He turned to jump on the window ledge.

"I see you all know each other," I said, "and Phoebe, you knew Deena was really a unicorn. Why did you call her a horse earlier?"

"Well, I didn't want the other gypsies to know she was a unicorn. As you know, only the pure of heart can see a unicorn in its true form. So now you know I am one of the good ones," she said with a grin as she went back outside to get something.

"We've all met here and there a couple of times." Deena said with a smile. "So, Sky, you are in these neck of the woods now."

"Yes and it was a good thing I was here," said Sky looking back at me. "I found your friend Murry down in one of the trapper's holes."

"Ahhh. They are at it again I see," added Deena.

"Just as I feared. This really isn't a safe place," said Glitz as he gathered our things together.

"What are you doing? We can't possibly leave this late. It's dangerous."

Phoebe came out with a horse and wagon. "I know this is not as fancy as the one you came with, but it will help get you where you need to go. I also packed some food for you," Phoebe said, handing me the horses' reins.

"Thank you very much. I am sorry we have to be leaving so soon." I said as Glitz began loading the wagon.

"It's okay. I understand. Glitz is right. This really isn't a safe place for you. Here," she said handing me a piece of paper.

"This is a map I think might get you where you want to go on your journey. I know you are not sure what you are looking for, but this may serve as a guide and, trust me, if there is somewhere you don't need to be or a place where you will be in danger, the things I have given you will let you know."

"Thank you," I said, giving her a hug. "I have a gift for you, too." I handed her a potted plant. "In this pot is a seed called the Murry Rose, and here are the directions on how to take care of it. With it you will be able to follow me on my journey. The rose will cast a shadow of me and whomever is with me. It will show you where we are and what or who we meet along the way."

As we were leaving, Deena walked up to Phoebe and whispered in her ear. Then she grabbed a small pocketknife and scraped some shavings off the unicorn's horn and put them into a pouch.

"What are you doing?" I asked.

"It's okay, Murranda," Deena whispered. "My horn has a lot of magic in it. And one thing it can do is make things grow faster. Many fairies possess the same magic as well."

"Yes they do," Glitz said sadly, looking to the ground. "But, not me. I really haven't discovered what magic I do have."

Deena helped Glitz into the wagon. "Don't worry Glitz. Your magic will be shown to you soon enough,"

"Deena let me ask you something. You say your horn can make plants and flowers grow faster, was it you that came to my house while we were all sleeping and made my mother's labyrinth garden grow?"

"You could say that," replied Deena with a bashful grin.

I was so happy that I gave her a huge hug. "I knew it was you. It had to have been. But why?" I asked.

"Does it really matter now?" she asked.

I shrugged my shoulders, "No, I guess it doesn't."

We gathered our belongings and gave Phoebe another hug, thanking her for all she had done for us.

"Please take good care of the rose," I said.

"And you take care of yourself and the others," Phoebe replied. "And don't worry, my new friends, we will meet again."

"I am sure we will," I agreed.

We settled into the wagon, waving good-bye as we got underway.

Even though we still did not know where we were going or what we were looking for, we felt certain there would be more excitement ahead for us.

What will we see? Who or what will we meet? But the biggest question of all is: *will I ever find what I am seeking?*

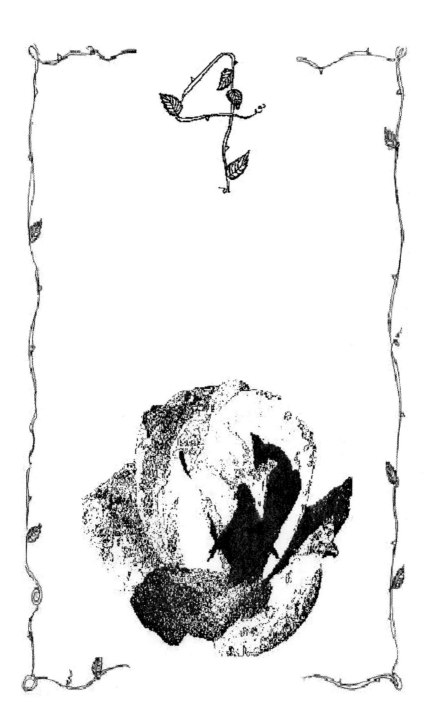

CHAPTER 4

Rudy spends his days and evenings sitting in the labyrinth garden with his pipe in one hand and a glass of bourbon in the other.

After he and Murranda had completed the garden, he built a small patio in the center of the labyrinth garden, right next to the Murry Rose. This is where he would sit and watch the shadow of his daughter in the center of the rose and see all that was going on with her.

Sometimes Rudy would also walk the labyrinth garden just as he did with his wife when she was pregnant with Murranda. This particular night he sat by the rose, staring at the shadow for hours while he held pictures of his departed wife, Morinda, and his lovely daughter, Murranda.

I should be there with my little girl. Why did I let her go on this crazy journey alone? He thought to himself. *Even though I know a fairy is with her, it still feels as though she is alone because I'm not there to protect her. She should never have left. She needed to stay here where it's safe.*

He worried about his daughter, knowing she had never been away from home this long.

Jeffery, came to the garden every once in awhile to check on his master and make sure he was okay. "Is there anything I can do for you Sir? "

"No thank you Jeffery unless you know a way of getting my Sunshine back home safely. In fact, why don't you sit with me for a while. Everyone else has left for the day, so it's just you and I. You have always been more than a servant to me Jeffrey. You are my friend. Pour us both a drink and have a seat here next to me while we watch Murranda and her friends. Maybe you'll be able to assure me I've done the right thing in letting her go."

"Thank you Sir, but if you don't mind my saying, I have known you since you were a little boy, and I watched you become a man. I recall the day you met Lady Morinda and the day your precious daughter was born. I also remember that tragic day you lost your beloved. I know how loving and caring you can be. I also know that you are a very strong and brave man, but if you don't mind me being bold, you can also be stubborn at times, Sir." Jeffery nodded as if to excuse himself, but continued.

"If you will recall, before your daughter was born, you and Lady Morinda would also go on many crazy, dangerous adventures. How many people tried to discourage you from doing all that you did. In fact, I also remember that even before you met Lady Morinda you would try to get me to join you," Jeffery added. "Your father and mine thought we were both crazy for doing all that we did, but yet you were so determined to prove to your family that you could do what you wanted and still be okay. "

"What are you trying to say?" Rudy interrupted with a smirk.

"Well, let me just say that young madam Murranda is a lot like you. She has that same stubborn, determined streak in her, but she is also as brave and gutsy as you are. You have to trust her and know that she will be okay—just like you were when you and your wife were her age. Let her have her own adventure like you did. Let her have her own journey. She will not put herself in any kind of danger that she cannot handle. Also, remember, she is not alone."

"Oh, am I supposed to take comfort in the fact that she is being protected by a fairy? What can fairies do?" asked Rudy.

"It's not what they can or cannot do, it's what they know and who they know. You would be surprised at what fairies can do and who they can call on for help," replied Jeffrey.

"I don't know Jeffery," Rudy said. "I understand what you are trying to say, but this is different. Murry doesn't even know where to look for what she is searching, and on top of that, she has no clue to WHAT she is searching for. She claims to have a feeling that she needs to find this thing, whatever this thing is."

"But Sir, did we always know what we were searching for or where we were going? No, we did not, at least not until the end. This is something young madam needs to do."

"Jeffery, you must remember what happened on the last adventure Morinda and I went on before she became pregnant with Murranda. I just don't want the same thing to happen to my little Sunshine. When her fairy friend Glitz was talking to me about the Shadow Land I remembered going there with my beloved and meeting the Dark Prince. I was about to put my foot down and tell her I forbade her to go." He took a long pull from his pipe.

"I will never forget that last adventure. Things may have turned out differently if we had not gone. Morinda might still have been with me today— raising our Sunshine together."

Jeffery let out a big sigh. "Yes, I remember that adventure and what took place. I too still think about that. But sir, you have to know, giving her your blessing to go on her one journey was the right thing. If you had not, she most likely would have gone anyway without your blessing. Wouldn't that have been worse?"

Rudy did not know what to say, so he sat there.

They both continued looking at the rose. They saw Murranda and Deena. "You see," said Jeffery, "she is not only with a fairy, now she also has a unicorn with her."

They also saw the gypsy fair. It looked as though Murranda was making friends with a gypsy lady. Then they saw the problem she had with the thieves who stole her carriage and belongings. That really worried her father. He gripped his glass of bourbon.

"Jeffery!" he cried. "Look at what is going on. You see, I knew I should not have let her go. I knew I should have gone with her or had one of the guards go with her."

"Sir, your daughter is fine," said Jeffery trying to calm Lord Rudy. "They took the horses and the carriage, but, as you can see, they did not take her. Trust me when I say I know she will be okay."

Rudy stood and began pacing back and forth across the garden, clutching the pictures; one of his beloved wife and a picture of Murranda. He looked at the picture of his wife and called out.

"Oh Morinda! Did I do the right thing by letting our only child go on this journey she so desperately wanted? She has never been away on her own before, and what did I do? I let her go to God knows where, and I have no idea when she will return. She doesn't even know what it's she is looking for. How could I have been such a fool of a father? Please my love, give me a sign that I haven't made a huge mistake. Can you give me a sign that you are watching over her from above? I promised you on your deathbed that I would always look after our daughter and keep her safe, but have I done the right thing by letting her take this journey to places she does not know, because she is looking for something she has to find, even though she does not know what it's she is looking for? Please give me any sign, I beg of you."

At that very moment, a gentle breeze brushed against his cheek. A peace came over him, as if his wife were saying, "Calm down my love. I am here."

He sat back down by the rose and watched. He saw when she fell into the deep hole. He saw Sky coming to her rescue. He thought to himself, *I do hope she will find friends along the way to help protect my Sunshine from any other dangers.*

Jeffery came and placed his hand on Rudy's shoulder. "You need to let her go and fly on her own to make her own adventures. Trust in yourself my Lord that you brought her up right and taught her well. If she is in real danger or if she is going to a place that we know she cannot defend herself against, we can then dig up the rose, put it in a pot and go find and help her. But let her try on her own first."

Even though Jeffery was trying to say the right things to make him feel better, he was still worried about his daughter.

"I will always worry about Murranda no matter how much training she has had. It's my right as a father to do so. Every father worries about his daughter no matter how old she becomes."

Rudy sat down with his drink in hand as Jeffery stood by him. Both of them watched the shadow in the rose.

CHAPTER 5

Back on the road, Glitz, Deena, Sky, and I continued on our journey following the map given to us by Phoebe. I had no idea where she'd gotten it, but she did claim to be a fortuneteller. Perhaps she had a vision of where we would be going next.

Whether we believed in her fortunetelling ability or not, we all agreed it was a good to follow her map instead of winging it. If I change my mind and decide to go a different route later, so be it. Since I don't really know where to look, some help was better than none.

As we continued on our quest I couldn't help but think about my father and how he was probably feeling. I was sure he would most likely be in the garden, sitting in front of the rose, staring at it and watching my shadow. I wondered if he had seen the people stealing our wagon and horses at the gypsy fair. Did he see us meeting Phoebe and Deena? I could only imagine how he would have felt if he had seen me fall into the animal trap where Sky rescued me. *I do hope he is okay*, I thought to myself.

"Your father is fine," said Deena.

"Excuse me!" I said. "How did you know what I was thinking? I didn't say that out loud."

"One of the abilities unicorns have is being able to read the minds of those we are close to."

"We can read thoughts, too," exclaimed Glitz. "I was about to tell you the very same thing."

"Well, that is not fair," I said with a smile. "Sometimes people like to keep their thoughts to themselves." We all laughed.

I looked over at Deena and asked, "You've known my family for years, right? Will you tell me some stories about my mother, maybe some things that my father may have left out? My father would tell me stories about how they met and stories about all the exciting journeys they went on, but I want to know stories about my mother when she was my age Will you please tell me all you know? Was she a sweet child? What kind of friends did she hang out with? Did she have a lot of friends, or was she like me with few friends. Was my father the only man she dated? What kind of student was she in school?"

"Slow down! Slow down my child," said Deena. "Our journey will probably be a long one, so we will have plenty of time to talk and stories to share. And yes, I had known your mother for many, many years, and I will be happy to tell you stories about her. She was a remarkable woman in her own way."

Down the road, Deena talked about what type of life Morinda had before she came to Xeenoephillia and before she met Father.

She told about Mother growing up in a village with many friends and about the man she dated before my father. I really liked that story. I thought I might bring it up next time I see my father. Deena said my father knew the man.

Deena also told me stories of how my mother first met the unicorns.

"On a journey when she was a child, she came upon a unicorn that had been tied up by trolls. She saw one of the trolls sharpening a large knife. She knew they were about to cut off the unicorn's horn because of the magic it held. So she very quietly crept up to the unicorn and untied it. The unicorn follow her into the bushes and far into the woods, and they were able to get away from the trolls. Because of that brave deed, all unicorns came to know her and befriend your mother. Once you save a unicorn's life it becomes your friend forever," explained Deena.

I couldn't get enough of the stories she told about my mother. I had always wished that Mother had not died when I was born so I could have gotten to know her myself, but with Deena relating the things she knew, I began to feel closer to her.

Glitz also told some fairy stories and even some stories of his elf friends. Sky told stories of his adventures and the curious creatures he became friends with. Some of their stories made me laugh. It was a lovely way to pass the time.

As we continued on, I could see that the clouds in the sky were getting dark and heavy. It felt as if a storm was coming.

Sky even lifted his nose in the air and sniffed. "I think we should take some cover and find shelter, friends. A big storm is brewing."

We all looked around, but couldn't find much in the way of shelter. Then I spotted an abandoned cave, just in the distance. It was big enough to bring in the horses and buggy that Phoebe gave us.

It looked old and run down and was a little damp and cold, but it was a lot better than being out in the storm. Sky was right. Within a few minutes the sky was full of lightning and thunder boomed so loud it made the ground shake. Glitz and I were somewhat afraid, but having Deena and Sky with made us feel a little better.

It was getting colder now, so we tried to build a fire. It was not a big one but it helped some. When the thieves stole our wagon they also took all our warm clothes and blankets.

"If you want, I can make my fur longer so you can all snuggle up to me. That would help keep you warm," said Sky as he started to grow.

At first Glitz was afraid of getting too close. "Don't worry Glitz, you will be okay around me. We don't eat fairies. In fact you are so tiny that we wouldn't even be able to taste you. Plus I consider you a friend."

"Well that is comforting to know, I guess." Glitz said as he wrapped himself around in Sky's tail.

"This is so cool!" Glitz and I said at the same time. We all gathered around Sky, snuggled up and went to sleep. It did help.

While I slept, I dreamt of the story Deena told about Mother saving the unicorn's life. In my dream, Mother and I were together. I was with Mother on one of her adventures. It was a pleasant dream. Suddenly I woke up to find to myself drenched.

"What in the world happened?"

Rainwater was coming into the cave. We had not realized that the cave was on a small hill, and it was such a strong storm, that rain was flowing in and making puddles.

"Come on guys. We really need to get out of here and try to find better shelter."

We climbed back onto the wagon and started off when we saw a small man just down the road waving his arms and yelling.

"This way, this way we can help you! We have shelter this way!"

As we got closer to him I could see he was a hobbit. We turned the wagon to follow him.

He led us to a little inn just past the edge of the tree line. "We have plenty of room here. We can take all your horses and put them in the barn with ours. Don't worry about your stuff, we will grab everything and take it inside. Your tiger and unicorn can stay with your horses in the barn," said the hobbit.

"I can shrink myself down to the size of a house cat," said Sky. And in an instant, he shrank to no bigger than that.

"Well now, ain't that the neatest thing ever. I guess now you can come in too. My kids would just love you," said the hobbit.

"Thank you very much," I said.

"Where are my manners? I am Wordorf Leadfoot," he said as he led us into the inn.

Another hobbit stood by a little fire, stirring a pot.

"This is my wife Helga," said Wordorf.

"Hello," she said. "Poor things, you are all soaking wet. And you, little one," she pointed to Glitz. "How can you even flap your little wings? Please come in."

She held out her hand for Glitz to land on. "I will take you all in and get you dried off near the fireplace. Then I'll get some warm clothes and food in you. Our people are feeding your unicorn and horses. They will be fine. I am sure we can find some dry clothes to fit you. If not, we can quickly make some," said Helga.

"My wife is the best seamstress in the village," explained Wordorf.

"Don't forget, I'm also the best cook," Helga added with a wink.

"Now how can I forget that my dear," Wordorf said as he patted his belly and leaned over to give Helga a kiss on the cheek.

I couldn't help but laugh at how cute the two of them were acting.

All of a sudden two little hobbits children ran up to us. "Yea, we have company. Look, they have a kitten we can play with."

"These must be yours," I said.

"Yes ma'am," they answered simultaneously.

"Why are all of you still standing around? Please make yourself at home. Here, have some warm apple cider. It will take the chill off." Helga said, handing us each a warm mug.

"Mama's cider can make anyone's bones warm and toasty," said the little girl. She gave Glitz a thimble size serving.

"What brings you out this way?" asked Wordorf.

"Well, first of all let me say thank you for your warm welcome and help, and also introduce myself and my friends. My name is Murranda, and the little fairy is Glitz. This is Sky and the unicorn outside is Deena. We are on a journey."

"A journey you say. What type of journey? What are you looking for?" asked Helga.

Glitz couldn't help but giggle. "We don't know what we are looking for or really where we are going."

"Now that is an interesting journey," said Helga. "Wordorf dear, don't you think our guests need to get out of their wet clothes and change into something warmer before we sit down for dinner?"

"We're okay. We don't want to be a bother. The cider is hitting the spot just right," I said, shivering.

"Kids!" Wordorf called. "Show our guests the washroom and where they will be staying. And see if you can pull out some things they can wear, maybe an outfit from your doll collection for Glitz."

"Actually, I can wear the little boy's clothes also," Glitz said raising his arms and bringing himself back to boy size. The hobbits were speechless. "Do it again, do it again," the little ones yelled.

"Now, now kids, these young ones are tired and most likely very hungry."

"Oh my word!" exclaimed Wordorf. "I have heard that fairies could do that. I just have never seen it done before. That is amazing!"

"You all go get cleaned up, including you my dear." Helga said as she gave her hubby a kiss and sent him on his way.

"Dinner should be ready soon. I should have it all set out by the time you all change into something warmer."

We all left to clean up and put on some warm, dry clothes. While I was in the bathroom washing my face the little girl came up to me with a brush in her hand. She stood shyly in the doorway.

"My name is Hanna. May I help brush your hair?"

"Hello Hanna, my name is Murranda, and you can call me Murry. Of course you can brush my hair. I would love that."

Hanna sat me down and stood behind me on a step stool and began brushing my hair. "You are very pretty, ma'am," she said.

"Thank you. So are you. How old are you Hanna?"

"I am 10 and my brother Hymes is also 10. We are twins. So, how long will you stay with us, Murry?" She asked as she kept brushing.

"Not very long. We have a very long journey ahead of us. We will most likely leave after dinner."

"Oh no, you must stay the night, it's so late and dark out there. If you have to leave, just leave tomorrow after a big breakfast. My mommy always says you can never really start a day without a good breakfast to get you going. Please won't you stay longer. My brother and I would love to ride your unicorn. We have heard so much about them. This is the first one I have seen in person. And your big cat, WOW! He is nice, isn't he?"

"Yes he is," I replied. "They are my friends. We really don't want to be a bother."

"Oh, I promise you won't be." Then Hanna called out "Mother?"

"Yes, my little one," Helga answered.

"Can Murry and her friends stay overnight? It's getting late and there is still a bad storm."

"Of course they are staying," Helga said with a giggle. "That is why I had you take them to their room. I have the beds already made."

"We really don't want to put you out," I said.

"You are not putting us out," Wordorf exclaimed. "It's settled. You are staying the night and telling us about your travels. How long have you been on this journey?"

"We haven't been on it very long." Glitz said. "So far we have come upon a gypsy fair and met a jewelry-selling fortune teller. We had our wagon stolen, but Phoebe, the gypsy, gave us hers to use. And that's where we met Deena and Sky. Before that, Murry and I made a labyrinth garden for her father and put the Murry Rose in the center of it. That is a flower she created which shows a shadow of her in the center so that her father can follow her on the journey."

"Oh dear, it sounds as though you have had a time of it. I am sorry to hear about your wagon being stolen. But, it was nice of your gypsy friend to let you use hers. This adventure you are on sounds like it's going to be unforgettable." Helga said as she fixed everyone's plate.

"Everything smells and looks so good. Thank you for doing all of this for us. You are all very kind," I said.

"You are lucky you didn't get hurt," said little Hymes. "I hear that gypsies can be dangerous."

Hanna tapped Glitz on his shoulder and said, "I picked some honeysuckles off a nearby bush. I can squeeze the juice out for you. I know fairies love honeysuckles."

"That's okay," said Glitz. "The best part about drinking the juice is getting it out yourself."

"That is our favorite thing to do, too," said Hanna and Hymes together. They began fixing a small dish of meat for Sky.

After dinner I helped them gather all the dishes and tried to help clean up.

"You don't have to do all this my dear, but I do thank you for your help." Helga said shooing me away from her kitchen.

I stretched and yawned. I guess I was more tired than I thought. We went to the room that the family had prepared for us. Fortunately, our room faced the barn where Deena was staying.

The room was big enough for all three of us to sleep. There were two small beds, one for me, and the other for Glitz. Sky slept at the foot of my bed. I could see through the window that Deena was looking to make sure we were all okay. I waved goodnight to her, blew out the candles on the nightstand and went straight to bed.

Early the next morning I heard quite a bit of commotion in the living room and kitchen. I looked over at Glitz and Sky. They were both still asleep.

I put on the clothes Helga had left at the end of the bed and went to see what was going on. She was pacing back and forth with a worried look on her face. Wordorf was coming in and out of the house. I went to Helga and put my hand on her shoulder.

"Is everything okay?"

"Yes, everything is fine," said Helga even though I could see that she had a worried look in her eyes.

"Please tell me what is wrong. I know something bad is going on," I said. "Maybe my friends and I can help you."

"Oh," she sobbed. "Everything is not fine. Last night's storm did a lot of damage to our village. All the crops were destroyed. We have nothing, and food is already getting more and more scarce."

"Really!" I said.

"Yes, you see this was not an ordinary storm. The Sorceress and the Dark Prince created it. They have wanted our land for years, for what I don't know. Some of the hobbits around here say that the Dark Prince wants to expand the Shadow Land. He hopes to make all of Xeenoephillia a Shadow Land and rule it all."

"That is awful!" I exclaimed.

"You're right, it's awful but not to worry my dear Murry," she said, toughening her face. "this has been our land for many, many years, so we are not about to let them have it. But, for now, we are paying the price for saying 'no' to them," explained Helga wiping the last of the tears and looking at all the devastation.

I went out to see what damage the storm had done to their village.

Everything was gone. Fences were knocked over or blown away. All the harvest was devastated. Most of the barns and homes were torn down or crumbled into bits. All of the livestock was running amuck.

I walked over to Deena. She was standing next to Wordorf and some of the other hobbit men. Sky awoke and came outside to see what was going on. He realized they needed our help and quickly grew himself to the size of a tiger. Some of the hobbits were a little afraid of him. We assured everyone that Sky was here to help.

Everyone talked about what they were going to do next, and wondered how they would be able to recover from this tragedy.

"This is really bad! Is there anything we can do to help?" I asked.

"Yes, it's very bad," echoed Deena.

I walked over to one of the hobbit men and asked if he had any of his seeds left. He nodded.

"Yes, but we will still miss harvest time. Autumn is almost over and then comes winter, so we will miss our harvest opportunity."

"We have to try. With the help of Deena, the unicorn, and her powers, maybe we won't be too late. We cannot let them win!" I said to the town hobbits as I stood on a pile of boxes.

"Who is willing to join me and try to make this work? Let's return this village to the way it was. No, even better!" I yelled.

"I will help you," said Glitz, as he came out of the house.

"So will I," said Deena "I have enough horn for all of you to shave and use to make your crops grow."

"Murry is right. We cannot let the Dark Prince and his Sorceress win. We have to stand and fight for our land," said Hymes.

"You are right son," said Wordorf. He stood proudly behind his kids with his arms around their shoulders.

Everyone in the hobbit village banded together to repair their damaged land. They gathered the horses they still had and used them to plow the fields. They gathered all the seeds that remained and planted them. Others gathered wood to fix the barns and houses.

The hobbit women also helped. Some corralled the run-away animals, while others cooked for the hard workers. Helga got one of her kitchen knives and started scraping some of Deena's horn to help the crops grow faster.

Glitz looked around. He knew they were going to need more help for the crops than Deena could provide. He went to the fairy bag he still had and pulled out his fairy flute. He shrunk back to his fairy size. He flew up to the tallest tree he could find and played it as loudly as he could.

I wondered what Glitz was up to. Then I heard the hobbit kids yelling and pointing. Out of the woods, a whole flock of fairies were flying our way, coming from all directions.

Glitz flew back to me.

"These are my friends. They can help with the crops and other things. Some of them are garden fairies and some are animal fairies. The animal fairies can help gather the animals and bring them back to the village and even get them to produce. They can get the chickens to lay eggs and the cows to produce milk. The garden fairies have the same abilities as Deena. They can help make the crops grow."

"That is great Glitz. Thank you." I said.

I watched what the fairies work, thinking of how sad the hobbits had been today. They awoke this morning to see their whole village destroyed. I wanted to do something more to help.

While the others were working on the village, I was in one corner of a small field working on making a labyrinth garden almost like the one my father and I made to honor my mother, but with a slightly different design.

I asked one of the children if there were any flower seeds. Hanna brought them to me, and I planted them along with some seeds I had left from my mother's garden.

When I finished, I took one of my Murry Rose seeds and planted it in the center of the labyrinth. I called out for Hanna to go fetch me something to write with and an old empty bottle with a cork. When she returned, I wrote instructions for how to care for the Murry Rose and explained its secret.

I rolled up the paper and stuck it into the bottle, placing it in the center with the rose. I then asked one of the children what day of the month it was, and a little boy said it was the 22nd. I took a small cup I found on the ground, went to the near-by well and got some water.

I tilted the cup so that it would make the water drip slowly, and counted 22 drops as it hit the spot where my Murry Rose laid. I called out to one of the nearby fairies,

"Can you help me make this garden grow. I wanted to plant some special flowers for everyone."

The fairy flew around and around the labyrinth sprinkling her fairy dust, and I could see all the flowers start to slowly grow.

After a several hours of our hard work with the help of Deena and the fairies' magic, the hobbits' village was restored better than before. The harvest was plentiful. All the barns and houses were repaired as good as new, and all the livestock were where they needed to be. Everyone was so happy that they celebrated with singing, dancing and a great feast.

It was getting late, so I gathered all my friends and let them know we really needed to be on our way. I went into the Leadfoot's inn to thank Helga, Wordorf and their children for their hospitality. I also thanked all the other hobbits for making us feel so welcome in their village.

I started to gather our thing to put in the wagon when I noticed something different about it. There was a wooden cover with a steel top on the wagon.

"We all wanted to thank you for the help you gave us in restoring our homes and village," said the oldest hobbit. "We noticed that you had no cover to protect all your belongings, so we made one for you with the wood and metal we had leftover. It's not much, but it might help. Now if you get caught in the rain and cannot find a village like ours, you can at least have some shelter from the rain."

"I packed you some more food left over from our feast. It should last you for a week or two," said Helga. She and the kids struggled to hold back the tears.

"Thank you for all your kindness. I truly hope you all do well," I said with a tear in my eye.

I saw Glitz talking to one of the hobbits. He gave the hobbit a flute of some sort then Glitz flew to the wagon.

"What were you doing?" I asked.

"Well, I saw that they were still very worried about their land, so I gave them one of my fairy flutes so they can call for help. Not only can it call the fairies, but also other magical beings like elfin warriors who can fight for them if needed."

I gave Wordorf, Helga and the kids a big hug and whispered to Hanna about the garden I planted. I told her to give the bottle with the note to her mother after we had gone.

"So, where to next?" asked Glitz.

"It looks to me that we need to go this way." I said pointing to the map.

Wordorf saw where I was pointing and said, "Oh that is the Mountain of the Two Sisters."

"Are you familiar with that area?" I asked.

"Yes I am, but you need to be very careful and try to stay out of the area between the two mountains," he said.

"Why? I asked.

"That is where the trolls live. In the Between," he explained.

"The Between? What is that?"

"You know, the Between; between two mountains or two bushes. They live between dark and light. Have to be careful. They are very tricky and dangerous creatures. They love to cause mischief and havoc wherever they go," he continued, "They will eat anything they can get their hands on, and that includes human flesh."

Glitz became frightened listening to Wordorf's warning about the trolls. He hid behind me in the wagon, even shrinking back down to fairy size. "They even eat fairies?" he asked, his voice wavering.

"As I said, they will eat anything," Wordorf continued. "But as long as you stay out of the 'Between' you should be okay."

"Honey, stop scaring them. They have a long journey ahead as it is," Helga said, putting her hands over Wordorf's mouth while she politely tried to change the subject.

"I saw the garden you planted for us. It's wonderful. Thank you."

Wordorf conceded to his wife, while she continued to ask about the flowers. "I noticed that the white one…the rose, had a shadow on it and according to your note, there is a special way we need to take care of it?" she asked.

"It's called 'The Murry Rose.' The shadow is mine. It will show you all that I am doing and who I meet along the way. I left instructions with Hanna." I explained.

"Wow! That is a special rose," Helga said. "We will be sure to take great care of it."

Glitz tugged at my pant leg and I realized we should be leaving. "Well, we need to be on our way."

We waved good-bye to all the hobbits. I couldn't help but smile thinking of all the things I have done and witnessed and the friends I had made so far along my way.

I wonder what is next for me? Who else will I meet? I thought to myself. Will they be as friendly, or as dangerous as the Dark Prince or the trolls I keep hearing about? Well whatever or whomever we meet we will be ready for it, I hope. No matter what, I am not going to stop looking for whatever it is I need to find. I hope it will be revealed to me soon. Every fiber of my soul is telling me not to stop looking for it. I just wish I knew what 'IT' was.

"Are you ready Murry?" asked Sky.

"Yes I am, let's go."

Sky and Deena guided the horses and the four of us headed towards the 'Mountain of the Two Sisters.'

CHAPTER 6

The four of us resumed our journey, and Deena continued with her stories about my mother.

"I cannot believe how much you know about my mother. Your stories are as amazing as the ones my father has told me. I am so happy I found you Deena. It's almost like having my mother with me on this journey."

As we walked through the trails toward the Mountain of Two Sisters, I couldn't help but ask, "why do they call this mountain the 'Two Sisters?'"

"Well, if I remember correctly," explained Sky, "it all started many years ago with two young orphans. They were living alone taking care of one another until one day, while walking through the woods they became lost and ended up in the Shadow Land. There, a family of vampires found them. You would think they would have just taken them and used them as dinner, but the legend says, the oldest female vampire begged the Dark Prince to let her raise them as her own."

"Wait! The Dark Prince is also a vampire?" I asked in shock.

"Yes, he is also a vampire," Sky continued. "As I was saying, at first the prince did not like the idea, but the female vampire convinced him that having the mortal sisters would be a great asset. They would be able to go back and forth from the Shadow Land to the human realm, bringing needed supplies and do other things vampires couldn't do. Plus, they could warn them of any coming danger. So the prince allowed her to raise the two sisters. She showed them the ways of the vampire world, their powers and the laws they had to obey. She also showed them all the other dark, evil creatures that inhabited the land."

"One of the sisters loved to learn all she could, while the other one knew it was wrong to be so evil and cause so much pain to others. Her conscience got the best of her, and one night she told her sister that she couldn't live with her in the Shadow Land any longer. She was going to run away and wanted her sister to come with her. But, the other sister loved all that she could do with the magic and the knowledge she possessed. There was no way she would ever leave what she felt was finally home for her.

They both understood each other's feelings. So, they kissed and hugged goodbye but decided to do one more feat of magic together. They made the mountain to remind themselves of how close they once were, knowing that the longer the one sister lived in the Shadow Land, the more evil she would become, and she would rule side by side with the Dark Prince."

"WOW! What a story," I said.

We noticed the sky was getting very dark in some areas, yet some areas were still light. It wasn't late yet, it was just getting dark, as if clouds were hovering above. I worried perhaps another storm was approaching.

"Sky, do you or Glitz know what is going on here? Why is it that one half of the trail is getting darker and darker and the other half is so light and beautiful?"

"Well, Murry," explained Sky, "the Mountain of the Two Sisters is right in front of the Shadow Land. The darkness is on the side facing the Shadow Land and the dark castle. The brightness, is the realms they haven't overtaken yet."

"I see. The Mountain of the 2 Sisters is what divides two parts," I exclaimed.

"You remember me telling you about the Shadow Land, don't you?" Glitz interrupted.

"Yes Glitz, I remember. What should we do? Should we go in a different direction?"

I stopped the horses and was about to turn around when something inside me stopped short. In my mother's journals, she always wrote that you should listen close to your inner voice, your gut feeling, because it would never steer you wrong.

Despite my fears and Glitz's warnings, I proceeded on towards The Two Sisters.

As we got closer to the mountain we could hear a strange sound, one I really can't describe. It was high-pitched, squeaky gibberish and what sounded like... hooting. I couldn't tell if someone was crying out in pain, or if it was an injured creature. The squeaky gibberish sounded like a foreign language of some sort.

"We are getting closer to the Between where the trolls live. I think that's them," said Glitz, nervously clutching my clothing.

As we got closer to the two mountains, we could see what looked like a dark hole with a glowing light in it, as if a campfire was glowing on the inside. The closer we got, the louder the sounds became. I have to admit I was getting a little scared, but I knew I needed to be brave and continue on.

We got off the wagon and tied the horses to the nearest tree, then walked slowly toward the direction the noises seemed to come from.

Just in front of us was a large pile of rocks like a part of a broken wall. Beyond the rocks was what looked like a miniature campsite. I gasped.

In the campsite were trolls. Some were singing and dancing while others were talking to one another. Then we heard a sound we couldn't quite make out. We peered over the rock pile and noticed several trolls sharpening knifes and axes. Others were stirring something in a huge pot over a fire.

Hanging above the pot was a large cage suspended by a thick rope. I couldn't believe my eyes! Inside the cage was an owl—a golden owl.

I remembered the story Glitz told me earlier. He was a bright golden color with emerald green eyes and onyx claws and beak. He was calling out trying to get the trolls to let him go. Three of them were poking at him through the cage with their spears.

"I have seen this owl times before," Deena whispered. "That's Cozmo. It figures," she said.

"What should we do?" I asked in a worried whisper.

"It looks as if they want to eat him, or maybe they will just melt his gold because they won't be able to eat him without breaking a tooth or two." She took a step back to get a better look.

"Right now his feathers look like regular feathers, but if someone pulls his feathers or he molts, they turn into 24 carat gold. If they kill him, he will become a 24 carat statue."

"We have to help him! We have to save him! We can't just let them kill the owl. There must be something we can do."

"Save him? Why? If we save him, he is going to be nothing but trouble." Deena said, rolling her eyes.

I couldn't believe what I was hearing.

"Deena, please, you know everyone is worth saving no matter how irritating they may be, and as you said before, he is not worth eating. Besides, I don't think those trolls know he is a golden owl."

"You're right about that Murry," said Glitz, "trolls are not the brightest creatures around. They're almost as dumb as giants. But, they are always mean and they are scavengers by nature. So, we need to be very careful. They aren't friendly at all."

"Well no matter what, we have to save Cozmo. There has to be a way," I said.

We snuck back to the wagon to formulate a rescue plan.

"I think I have an idea on how to do this," said Sky. "I will go there as a small kitten and walk around. They'll think I'm a snack. With every step, I will grow slowly larger and larger until all the trolls will realize just how much of a meal I could be. I'll keep them busy enough to forget about the owl. You can go around to the other side, untie his cage and bring him to the wagon."

"But what about you, Sky? We don't want you to become their dinner," I said as I knelt down to pet and hug him.

"Don't worry Murry. Trust me when I say, I can handle a few trolls. I have dealt with these buggers before. It's almost like a game for me." He rubbed my cheek with his face.

"Plus, you forget just how big I can get. I can get so big they will change their minds about eating me. That is where the true game begins. Don't worry. If I have to flatten a few trolls, so be it! That is just one or two less trolls to deal with in the balance of all that is evil."

"Please Sky, be careful, and try not to hurt anyone if you don't have to."

"Okay, I'll *try* to be good," he said, moving into position behind the wall. "But, you're taking all the fun out of this."

We followed Sky toward the campsite and hid behind the rock pile. Meanwhile, the owl was going on and on.

"I see someone told you Neanderthals that I was more fun than you could shake a stick at," he screeched. "So, you decided to POKE fun at me." The trolls just grunted.

"And being the overgrown kindergarteners that you are, you wanted a captive audience, hence you stuffed me in this stupid cage. Look," he pleaded, "if you just knock it off I will lay you a golden egg, and then you can buy as much food and stuff as you want. But first, you have to let me out of here. I need some time to build a nest in private. Do you honestly think I can actually do that with a crowd watching? Please, I promise! If you let me out I will get started and lay an egg for you, maybe even two."

We could hear his sad pleas to the trolls. As pathetic as they were, we had to cover our mouths so as not to laugh out loud.

"I think you are right Deena. He does seem a little full of himself. He might be trouble." Deena nodded her head.

I looked over at Sky to see if we were ready for 'Operation Save Cozmo.' Sky nodded his head.

He walked towards the campsite catching the attention of the younger trolls. They followed him, just as he said they would.

The female trolls had little outfits in their hands. Oddly, they tried to put them on Sky.

"Yea, Kitty, Kitty," they yelled.

With each step he took, Sky got a little bigger and a little bigger till you could hear the kids yelling, "Ohhh, big kitty, big, big kitty."

He grew even bigger, to the point he frighten the kids. "No! Kitty too big, too big."

The little ones ran towards the bigger ones. They turned their attentions to Sky, who by now had become huge, gray, and tiger-like. They looked back at the owl in the cage. Realizing Sky would make a much better meal, the trolls grabbed whatever they could find to chase him.

Sky ran from the campsite. All the trolls followed. As planned, we moved to the other side to rescue the bird.

I untied the rope from the pole and grabbed the cage, sliding it onto Deena's horn. I could see her rolling her eyes again. Once I got the owl away from the campfire, we ran back to our wagon.

"We've got him. Let's go!" I said.

While we were running, the owl yelled "Ah, I am a male owl. I cannot even lay eggs you stupid trolls! Ha, ha, ha! I tricked you, didn't I?"

"Shut up!" I said. "In case you haven't noticed, we are trying to save your feathered butt. So if you don't mind, zip it!"

Cozmo ruffled his feathers and said, "Save me? Save me? I didn't need your help. I had those stupid wrinkled walking raisins right where I wanted them."

. "Well, if he thinks he doesn't need our help, why don't we just put him back so he can do the job himself?" Deena said.

I turned back toward the troll's campsite.

"Well, wait a minute," Cozmo said, debating his quandary. "Since you have already gone through the trouble of rescuing me, I guess we could go somewhere a little safer than this," he said with a crooked grin, "but just so you know, I did have them right where I wanted them. I know I did."

Deena gave a big sigh and rolled her eyes once more as we headed back toward the wagon. I jumped in, and Deena tilted her head down so I could get the cage off her horn.

I grabbed the reins and told the horses to go. When I looked back for Glitz and Sky, I saw Glitz flying our way. When he reached us he perched himself on my shoulder.

"Where is Sky?" I asked, looking around for him.

"Sky is okay. He is having fun chasing the trolls away. He will be along soon. You should have seen him Murry. He is so good at this. He is jumping over huge rock piles and climbing and jumping from tree to tree and over hills. He is getting those silly trolls so confused they don't know where they are."

"Oh please, those brainless idiots! Anyone can confuse a troll. They get confused just by watching a leaf fall from a tree." Cozmo retorted as he tried to clean himself.

"I couldn't believe they thought they could eat me. They would have broken a tooth or two on the first bite."

"Shhh," I said, "I think I see something."

Sky was head back towards us. It did not look like he was being followed.

"Sky, are you okay?"

"I am fine, but you need to get going. We all need to get away from here as soon as possible. Once the trolls get tired of chasing me, they are going to figure out how to get back to the campsite and see that the owl and the cage are gone. Then they are going to be angry and start hunting, and that is going to be an even bigger mess." Sky quickly shrank himself back down and jumped into the wagon.

"Now I want to see this golden owl we have heard so many stories about," he said, looking Cozmo over.

"I cannot believe you truly exist. All this time I thought the stories were made up by people to amuse their kids."

"Well, you over-grown fuzz ball, as you can plainly see, they were not. My name is Cozmo, and you are?" he asked, fluffing his wings.

"Well, my name is Murranda, and this is Glitz," I began, pointing to each one. "This is Sky and this is De…"

"Oh, I know who this hay bag is," Cozmo quickly interrupted. "So Deena, we meet again."

"Watch it, you walking 24 carat feather duster," Deena said with a snarl. "You could have at least thanked us for saving your hide."

"Okay, thank you, thank you! Are you happy now? Now if you don't mind, can you please get me out of this cage, and I will tell you all about myself," Cozmo said as he tried to unlock the cage with his claw.

I was about to open the cage to let him out when Glitz stopped me. "Why don't you first tell us about yourself, then we will let you out."

"Very well, if that is how you want to be," Cozmo said with a heavy sigh.

"My name is Cozmoneus O'Brian"

"Oh, so you are Irish." I said with surprise.

"Yes, I am Irish," Cozmo said, rolling his eyes.

"I only meant that to say you don't have an Irish accent," I explained.

"Yes, she is right," said Sky. "O'Brian is a very strong Irish name. Normally someone with that name would have a strong Irish accent. So, what happened?"

"Okay, I am not 100% Irish, but that is not the issue here. If it will make you all happy, I could talk like this," he said with an Irish accent. "Do you want to know about me or not? You can just let me go for all I care."

I put my hands in front of Cozmo and Sky and said, "Okay, okay, let him continue. Go ahead Cozmo. Please continue."

"Let's see, where was I? Oh yes, not only am I Irish, but I was once also human, believe it or not. Let's just say my Irish luck ran out. Pardon the pun. I was once a tax collector for the king of Xeenoephillia. Well at least that's what I made him think. I would give myself a few bonuses here and there when he was not looking. You know, take from the top." He widened his feathers to show just how much he took.

"I mean, who wouldn't do that? The king had more money than he could count. I also convinced a sorceress to help me do what I needed to do in order to become as rich as the king. Even though she did not want to, I had ways of getting what I wanted." He paused to shake his feathers.

"She kept saying that I was too greedy and that my greed would get the best of me—whatever that meant. But then she decided to play a cruel joke and turn me into what she said I craved the most. She was a clever sorceress that one, putting some kind of magic elixir into my nightcap. The next morning I woke up in feathers with a note by my bed. Now I every time I molt or someone tried to pluck my feathers off they turn into gold bars. She also wrote something about the only way I would be able to break the spell was to do a selfless act. Trust me, I have tried, but I am still a bird."

While Cozmo was telling his story, I heard a clunking sound against the wagon floor. I looked around, and Cozmo was bleeding. As soon as the blood hit the wagon, the droplets turned to rubies.

"You're hurt Cozmo."

Cozmo looked at what I was pointing to and said, "Oh I suppose I am. I guess one of those trolls must have gotten me with the skewer."

I looked into the bag Deena had given me earlier. I found a blouse and tore a piece from it to make a makeshift bandage. I gave it a little pressure.

"OUCH! Watch what you are doing little girl. That hurts!" yelled Cozmo.

"I am trying to stop the bleeding."

"Okay, I did my part. Now if you don't mind, please let me out," he said impatiently. "A bird like me is meant to be free."

"But you are hurt, Cozmo. I truly think you need to stay in the cage till that heals," I said, still concerned.

"LOOK," Cozmo exclaimed, "I have been on my own for quite a while now. Through all that time, I have learned to take good care of myself. So if you don't mind, just let me out. Thank you for your so-called help, but I've got to fly."

"You don't have to be rude," said Glitz folding his arms and getting between Cozmo and I.

"Look here, you overgrown fly in a suit. I told you my story, and you said you would release me once I did."

"Guys, he is right. We did promise. I guess a promise is a promise," I said, reluctantly unhooking the cage.

Cozmo slowly stuck his head out to look around and climbed out of the cage. "Thanks for your hospitality, but this golden bird is out of here," he said.

He spread his wings, but it was clear he was having trouble flying. He winced in pain and the blouse bandage I made for him was leaking.

Blood began to fall. Tiny rubies rained against the ground.

"I don't think he is going to get very far," commented Deena. "Unless he can get that bleeding to stop, he is most likely going to get caught once again."

"Again?" I asked. "You're telling me that Cozmo has been caught more than once?"

"What did you think Murranda? He is an owl made of gold and gems. A lot of people want him. It's kind of ironic if you think about it," Deena said.

"When he was human, all he wanted was money, gold, and gems, and now that he is made of gold and gems, everybody wants him."

Part of me wanted to follow him and convince him to stay with us till he was healed. But, when I looked up, he was long gone.

CHAPTER 7

    Everything around us was getting darker and darker. "It looks like night time is approaching here quickly."

"It's not night," said Sky. "We are approaching the Black Forest."

"The Black Forest?"

"Yes, we must be extremely careful. We're getting closer to the Shadow Land, but this is the only way we can go without going back to the trolls."

Suddenly, Glitz pointed to my neck yelling, "Murry, Murry, your necklace. It's gone. Where is it?"

I put my hand on my neck and felt for it. "Oh no, it must have dropped when we were saving Cozmo. We have to go back and try to find it."

"Do you really want to go back there, knowing they are looking for the owl? If they see you they will think you have him," cautioned Sky.

I didn't know what to do. Part of me that wanted to go back, but the other part of me wasn't so sure the necklace was really worth it. I know what Phoebe said, but I made my decision. We needed to travel onward.

Suddenly we heard a whistling sound coming from the distance. I turned around to see where it was coming from, and I heard Deena yell, "MURRANDA WATCH OUT!"

I felt a sharp pain in my left shoulder and chest. I had been struck by an arrow!

The last thing I heard was Glitz yelling, "Murry, Nooooo…"

I must've passed out.

Glitz was yelling. "Somebody help her. Murry has been hurt." Glitz and Sky grew full size and along with Deena, they formed a circle around me for protection.

Even though I was semiconscious, I could still hear bits and pieces of what was going on. I couldn't tell if it was real, or if I was in another dream. I remember hearing a voice I did not recognize. *Don't worry, I am here.*

At first I thought it was Mother's voice. What is going on?

Hurry, we must get her out of here, the voice said. I was worried that Father was watching the rose and seeing what was going on. He must be freaking out about now. He most likely is trying to find some way of reaching me. I wondered if Dee Dee and Flutter or the Hobbits were doing the same thing. What if Phoebe, my gypsy friend, was watching? Did she see this coming? Is she angry that I lost the necklace that was supposed to protect me?

I finally opened my eyes. Immediately, I felt an intense pain in my shoulder and chest. I looked and saw the arrow that had pierced my shoulder was still in me.

"Where am I? How did I get here? What happened? Where is everyone?"

"Don't move," said a young girl with pointed ears. I recognized her as an elf, but where had she come from? And where was everyone else?

She was slender with long dark brown hair and dark eyes. "Please don't move. You need to stay perfectly still," she said. "Don't worry. You will be okay. The arrow did not get your heart. It's just above it. We will take all of you somewhere much safer than this."

"Who did this to me? And why?"

"Don't worry about that. My brother and I are going to find out who did this."

"Who are you?" I asked. "Where is it that you are taking us?"

"My name is Nessa. We are taking you to Elfinnia, the forest of elves. You are in the dark forest now. Our land is just on the other side. You will be safer there. You most likely got hit by one of the dark elves' arrows. They are hunters for the Dark Prince and the Sorceress. Hurry! We have to get out of here."

Sky appeared and grew so I could ride on his back while Nessa held me.

"You will be fine," she said. "Your wagon was destroyed. The dark elves shoot fire arrows too, your wagon burned to the ground."

"No!" I yelled.

"Let's go to Elfinnia," said Nessa.

"Oh Murry," whispered Glitz. "Are you okay?"

"Not really, Glitz. I am felling sick, and my vision keeps going in and out."

"It's the poison from the arrow," interrupted Nessa. "Once we get back to my home we will help you."

"Oh Murry," said Glitz, "I wish this had not happen to you. I wanted to bring you to Elfinnia in a better way. I know these elves…"

I was not paying much attention to what Glitz was saying. I kept thinking I was seeing my mother walking toward me or, I was back home with Father. It had to be the poison that was making me feel and see things.

"We are almost there. Just hang on and stay awake," said Nessa. "Glitz, keep talking to your friend. Make sure she does not fall asleep until we can get her to see my brother, the wizard elf."

I heard two voices saying, "They are over here. No, they are over here." I drifted in and out finally waking up to a bright round bubble light above me coming slowly toward me.

"Who are you?" I asked.

Glitz looked up to where I was pointing and asked, "Who is who, Murry? What do you see? I don't see anything. Are you okay? Wake up Murry! Don't go to sleep. You are just seeing things. Everything is going to be okay."

"Glitz don't you see it? It's right there. It's so beautiful!"

I saw slender shape with what looked like long black hair, but I couldn't see a face. The light around it was so immensely bright I couldn't look directly at it. I couldn't even tell if it was male or female. All I could see was such beauty, just pure beauty.

I closed my eyes for a bit to catch my breath, and when I opened them, it was gone. "The person in the bubbled light, where did they go?"

"Where did what go?" Glitz questioned. "Nothing is there Murry. You are going to be okay."

"We are almost at the forest of elves. You must keep calm or the poison will spread faster through your body," said Nessa, guiding us forward.

I passed out again.

When we arrived at Elfinnia, they brought me into a room. I opened my eyes again and saw what look like the most beautiful and magical tree house I had ever seen. There were crystal and gold and emerald leaves hanging everywhere. I looked at my shoulder and saw the arrow had been removed. My mouth tasted like I had swallowed wood. I spit and rubbing my mouth trying to get the taste of wood chips out.

"So, I see you finally decided to wake up," said a male elf as he walked toward me with a cup of something.

"Drink this. It will help with the pain," he said. "We had them put a strong piece of wood in your mouth to bite down on when we pulled out the arrow. You passed out. The good news is you are going to be just fine. We got the poison out just in time. However, you are still weak and must rest to regain your strength."

I looked on the floor and saw that I'd lost a quite a bit of blood. I drank the elixir as best I could. It had a strong bittersweet taste, kind of like unripe berries. It was hard to drink because it was very thick.

"Thank you for saving my life. My name…"

"…I know. You are Murranda. Your friends were here to assist me in getting the arrow out. I am Evanwood, the wizard elf."

He was a young, blond-headed, bearded elf, wearing a blue and green robe with a crystal hanging around his neck. "I see you have already met my sister, Nessa, and this is my brother, Jett."

As he was speaking, a young well-built elf entered the room with arm armload of bandages and a bow and arrow strapped to his back.

"Here Evan, these are the bandages you asked for." Jett stopped to give me the once over.

"So you are the one that is causing all the fuss around here! Evan, why do you always want to help these humans when all they do is destroy our land to gain more property and money for themselves and their kingdoms? No one cares about the animals and nature here, so why should we care about them?" Jett raved.

"You're wrong Brother. Murranda and her friends were not destroying anything. They were minding their own business—the Prince's elves did this. I don't believe this girl is here to destroy anything." Evanwood said.

"Well, I still think humans are not worth helping if they are not going to help us," replied Jett.

"I am sorry for whatever my people have done to you, but I am not that way. I have always put nature and animals first," I softly added.

"She is right, Jett," Nessa said as she walked in. "She is on our side. This human is pure of heart."

"Maybe so, but I will still keep my eye on this one," he said storming out of the room.

"Don't worry about my brother. He is mostly all talk. He is just very protective of this land. More and more of Elfinnia is getting destroyed."

Nessa rubbed a wet leaf on my head before redressing my wound. When she took the old bandage off, I could see that my shoulder was black and blue with a dark hole between my shoulder and chest. It still hurt quite a bit, but not as much as before. I looked around for my friends and couldn't see anyone.

"Where are my friends?"

"Don't worry. They are outside getting their rest. They are telling us about what you are doing, about this journey you are on, and how you are looking for something. I think that is so exciting," exclaimed Nessa.

"They have told us about your experiences so far and about a rose that you have made which can allow the owner to follow you on your journey. They said your father was one of the first to have one of the special roses. I hope he can see that you and your friends are okay now."

"I'm sure he has been watching the rose, and he most likely is very worried because of what he has seen so far," I replied. I rubbed my shoulder and tried to sit up.

"I want to thank all of you for everything you have done, especially for saving my life."

"I know you want to continue on your journey, my child," Evanwood said as he helped me up. "But you really must rest until you have regained your strength. As you can tell, there are powerful evil forces out there, and you must find more ways of protecting yourself and your friends."

"I had a necklace. It was supposed to warn me of danger, but I lost it." I said, putting my hand on my neck.

"Did your protection necklace have anything that came with it like a bracelet or ring?" he asked.

I nodded and showed him my ring.

"I may have a way of getting your necklace back if they really belong together."

Evan held out his hand, and I placed the ring on it. He then made a circle on the table next to me with some red and black powder.

He placed the ring in the center of the circle. He gave me a piece of chalk, and asked me to draw the necklace.

"Think hard about the necklace, as if it was right in front of me," he said.

It was hard to draw the necklace because of my injured shoulder, but I did the best I could, and before I finished, it appeared on the table.

"Wow that is amazing! Thank you."

"I truly did not do much. You did most of it. You see, Murry, the ring and the necklace are one. If you lose them, repeat this act and they will come to you. But your necklace or ring is not enough to protect you from the dark forces out there. You and your friends must learn to protect yourselves. So I insist that you and your friends stay here until you are well and have the proper training and tools to do battle when necessary."

"According to what your fairy friend has told us, you really have no need to hurry since you don't know what you are looking for or where it is," said Nessa.

I thought about it and agreed. "Evan, can I ask, why did the dark elf try to kill me?"

"I don't really think they were trying to kill you. If that were the case, you would be dead. I just think they wanted to capture you, maybe for the necklace and ring. Where did you get them?" Evan asked.

"A gypsy named Phoebe gave them to me," I said.

"Mmm, I wonder? Never mind, it does not matter now. You need to rest. You and your friends must be hungry. I will help get you down from here so you can join your friends at the feast. You are about to witness an elfin celebration."

"What kind of celebration?" I asked.

"It's a celebration we have when young elves finally discover what their gifts are. This determines what kind of elf they will become. It happens every blue moon to all elves that are 16—in human years that is. The Blue Moon Goddess prepares several tests that will determine each young elf's special gift." As she explained, Nessa helped me dress in an elfin outfit.

"This should fit you and be more comfortable for moving around with your injury."

"Thank you," I said as I tried to put on my necklace.

"Here, let me help you," she said. As she put her hands near my neck to clasp the necklace, I peered through the door and noticed how high we were.

"How are we going to get down from here? Or should I say, how did you get me up here?"

"Like this," said Evan.

A cage rose from the floor. Nessa and Evan opened the door. Once we were inside, Nessa and Evan maneuvered some rope to take us down.

At the bottom, they helped me out of the cage and led me to a table loaded with food. Before we sat, Evanwood handed me a small vial of elixir and asked me to drink it. "This should allow you to move without hurting."

"Thank you Evan, but it's not hurting that much anymore."

"Really? May I take a look at your wound?" he asked with a puzzled look on his face.

"Sure," I said, and I opened up part of my dress to expose my left shoulder where the bandage was. He removed the bandage to see that the wound was almost healed.

"Nothing in my medical bag would do this. Are you sure you are not part elf or part magical being?" he asked.

"No, I am just a girl."

"Then it must be the necklace," said Nessa. "It's supposed to protect her from harm. Or maybe it's the ring."

"It was me! I did it!" Glitz said as he flew over to me and changed back to child size.

"When you were getting things ready for the feast, I flew up to check on her. I remembered what the gypsy woman gave me. I poured a drop onto her wound to see if I could help her. And look, it's working!"

"That is some magic you have there my little friend. Can I see the vial you used on her?" Evan asked.

Glitz took the small vial out of his pocket and showed it to Evan.

He opened it and said, "Just as I thought. Do you know what you have here Glitz?"

He shook his head. "What you have in this vial is Elvin tears. An elf's tear can cure almost anything. I was going to give you the same thing once I got you back in your room and checked your wound. The gypsy that gave you this vial and gave Murry the necklace and ring must be one of the orphan sisters--Phoebe. She has been living among elves since she left the Shadow Land." Evan explained.

Glitz and I just looked at one another then back at Evan. "You know the story of the Mountain of the Two Sisters?"

"Yes," I replied.

"Well, Phoebe—the one who gave you this I presume, is the good sister. Pheonna, her twin is Sorceress of the Shadow Land. It's all beginning to make sense now! Pheonna must know that the necklace and ring are near. It's why you were attacked. She wants them. She is very aware of the powers they possess."

I did not know what to say.

"You see, Brother, I told you we should not have gotten involved. Now she is bringing evil back to our forest," said Jett.

"Jett, just sit down and be quiet. Murry has nothing to do with Pheonna's rage. We will help her and her friends."

Jett couldn't take any more. He angrily left the table and busied himself helping the younger elves. The rest of us sat down to eat, and Deena and Sky finally came to join us.

"Oh Murry, I am so happy to see you up and about. How are you feeling?" Sky asked.

He rubbed against my left side.

"OUCH... I was fine until now. Thanks." I said, wincing as I began to scratch behind his ear with my right hand.

"Oh, I am sorry. Wrong side," he said.

"That's okay. Where have you guys been?"

"We went looking around to see if we could find your necklace," said Deena. "But I see that you have already found it."

"Yes, thanks to Evanwood."

After dinner, the elves threw quite the celebration. The Blue Moon Goddess descended from the sky. She was so breathtakingly beautiful. Her skin glistened in the moonlight, and her hair was long and blond. She wore a dress with all shades of blue that accentuated her eyes, which were bluer than mine.

There was so much food, great music and lights. I really enjoyed watching the Blue Moon Goddess work with the young elves. They went through their different challenges to discover their unique gift. Some learned they were fierce warriors while others found out they were wizards. Some of the elves possessed the gift of healing while some could talk to animals and plants. It was amazing! I began to wish that I had those gifts. They could truly come in handy on my journey.

"Are you enjoying the celebration?" asked Nessa.

"Oh yes, this is so much fun. Thank you for allowing us to be a part of it."

"The pleasure is all ours. But you must know a few things about what you are wearing. The necklace and ring are two of the most powerful weapons you have to fight against the dark forces you will face. Pheonna and the Dark Prince have been after them for years. In the right hands they can be used for great things, such as healing and protection from all that is evil." She glanced over at her brothers.

"In the wrong hands," she continued, "they can bring destruction and devastation to all of Xeenoephillia. This is the battle between good and evil, and now you and your friends are in it. As long as you have this necklace and ring, your lives will most likely be in danger."

"Then she should get rid of it," said Glitz pulling at the necklace.

"STOP Glitz! I have to wear this. Don't ask me how I know, but I have to. I am not scared of what is out there. They have already come for me with a poison arrow, what could be worse?"

"Do I have to answer that?" Glitz said as he stared me in the eyes.

"The elves are going to teach us some battle techniques, so we can learn to fight what is out there. The ring and necklace will help us. We will be okay."

I kissed Glitz on the forehead to comfort him.

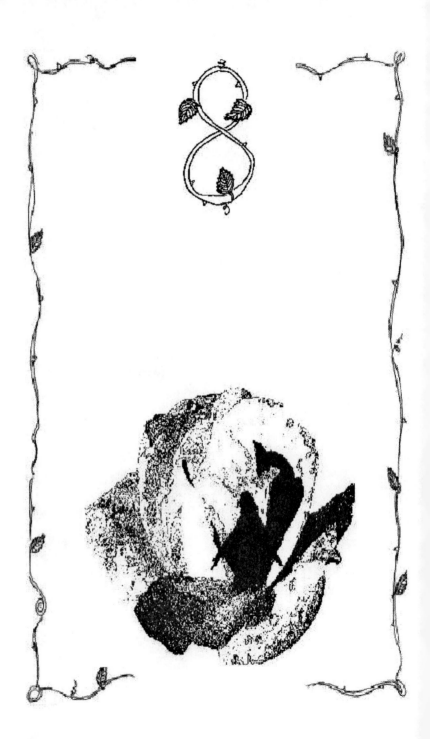

CHAPTER 8

Back at the gypsy village, Phoebe was in her carriage house eating dinner and watching her Murry rose. She could see everything that had been going on. She saw how we arrived at the hobbit village and what happened there. She saw how we saved the owl from the trolls. But what worried her most was what happened to me afterwards, when I was struck by the poison arrow. Phoebe knew who was responsible.

"I cannot believe it. She must know that the necklace and ring are nearby. She can feel it. I need to get to Murranda and her friends. They need me. They are no match for my sister and the prince."

As Phoebe quickly started packing, another gypsy came calling.

"What are you doing? Where are you going?"

"Hi Serena," Phoebe said, waving her hands, "I am sorry but I have to leave. I cannot tell you much, just know that I will be okay, and I'll be back as soon as I can,"

As soon as she stepped outside Phoebe suddenly stopped in her tracks. A vision came to her.

She could see two men in a large house; one looked like a servant the other reminded Phoebe of Murranda. It must be Murry's father, she thought.

The two men looked very worried and were getting some things together. One of the men dug up a another Murry Rose and put it in a pot to carry. Then they stormed out the door.

The vision took Phoebe's breath away. Luckily Serena caught her just before she fell.

"Are you okay? Did you have a vision?"

"Yes I did," Phoebe said.

She turned back into her place and put everything down. "I think it's best if I stay here. I think I am going to have some company. They may need my help, too. I have to find a way to guide them here."

Phoebe picked up her Murry Rose and lightly touched the petals. She closed her eyes and focused on the two men with the rose and also on Murranda.

Meanwhile, Rudy and Jeffery were in one of their carriages riding to find Murranda.

"I cannot believe I let her go. Now she might die. I could lose her too," Rudy repeated.

"You won't, Sir," Jeffery said. "We will find her."

"How? We have the rose, but it does not give us a map. She is out there somewhere in pain with an arrow in her chest." Rudy said in frustration.

He stopped the carriage and sat there, staring into space. He remembered the things he had seen in the rose before, and started to have visions of Murranda and Glitz at a gypsy fair.

"Jeffery," he said, "do you remember when we looked at the rose the last time and saw my daughter and Glitz at some kind of fair? I think it was a gypsy fair."

"Yes Sir, I do remember that, and I know where there is one this time of year."

"Well then man, what are we waiting for? You have the reins, let's go!"

At the gypsy village, Phoebe sat with Serena, waiting. "I think it's working Serena. I sense them coming this way. I suppose I should straighten up a bit. We will be having company soon."

"Wow Phoebe! Your powers are truly growing."

"Now if I can only find a way to let Murranda know what is going on. Maybe if I can get her to dream—but she is so far away, and I don't think she has her rose with her, just the seeds."

"Is there some way you can send a message, perhaps?"

"Yes, that's a great idea."

Phoebe began writing. As soon as she had penned the letter to be sent, a young girl came in to drop off some papers for Phoebe. The girl was slender with long dark brown hair and dark brown eyes with some red in them. Her clothes were worn and dirty and she was also bare foot.

As the young girl handed the papers to Phoebe, their hands touched creating another, even more startling vision for Phoebe.

"Little one, what is your name?" Phoebe asked.

"My name is Phoenix, ma'am, like the bird." The young girl said.

"You are not truly a gypsy, are you?"

"Ma'am?" Phoenix asked quickly backing towards the door.

"Don't worry my friend. I won't say anything. Where are you from? How did you get here?"

"I am an orphan. My parents are dead, and the old lady I was with couldn't continue caring for me, so she left me here with the gypsies. I help out however I can in exchange for food and shelter."

"I am sorry to hear about your family, but you can do me a big favor. It may be dangerous, but I can pay you, and give you some things that might help you on your way. I need you to deliver an urgent message to a young girl named Murranda. She is traveling by wagon with a horse, a charma cat and a fairy boy named Glitz."

"I am not afraid of danger. I kind of like to get into things. Where is the letter going?"

Phoebe looked back at the rose to see if she could tell where Murranda and her friends were. She remembered seeing them save the owl near the mountains. The new shadows showed elves. Perhaps they had made it to the Forest of Elves.

"Do you know where the Mountain of the Two Sisters lies?" she asked Phoenix.

"Everyone who lives in Xeenoephillia knows the Mountain of the Two Sisters," Phoenix laughed.

"Then you must also know the Elvin forest."

"Oh you mean Elfinnia? Yes, I know where that is. Is that where your friends are?" asked Phoenix.

"I believe so. Can you go now and deliver this message? Find the elf wizard, he may be able to help you. Also, I want you to wear this." Phoebe handed Phoenix a necklace with a tiger's eye. "It will protect you, and it will let me know when you have reached Murranda and her friends."

"Thank you ma'am," Phoenix said as she put the necklace on and placed the letter in her pocket.

"Please, since you are doing this for me, I consider you a friend so call me Phoebe. And be careful. If by any chance you get lost or need help, close your eyes and rub the stone. I will be there to help you."

She kissed Phoenix on the forehead. Phoenix nodded her head, and started on her way.

"Do you think she will find your friends, Phoebe?" Serena asked.

"I pray she does Serena. Murranda needs to know that her father is not just sitting at home watching her in the Murry Rose. She needs to know he has seen her in harm's way. I also hope Murranda's father will find us soon. Maybe I can persuade him to delay his search and just let her continue on the journey alone. She is in a safe place for now, but that will change when Murranda realizes she is destined to enter the Shadow Land. If I know my sister, she is not going to give up. She wants the necklace and ring, and both she and the prince will stop at nothing to get them."

Back at the hobbit village, Helga Leadfoot was in the garden Labyrinth watering the flowers. When she got to the center, where the Murry Rose was, she saw all that was going on with Murranda and her friends. She cried out to her husband.

"Wordorf, come here quickly. It's Murry. They are in trouble."

"Murranda? Where is she? Are they back already?" He asked running towards his wife.

"No, the rose is showing that someone has shot her with an arrow," replied Helga, putting her hand on her chest as if to hold her breath.

"I can't tell how badly she is hurt, but I do see that she has met some new friends, and they are helping her."

"I hope they are friends. It looks as if her journey may be more than she bargained for. I hope this thing she is looking for is worth all that she is going through," said Wordorf

He stood back and put his arms around Helga.

"I just pray that she will be okay," said Helga.

"So do I, my dear. So do I."

CHAPTER 9

Back in Elfinnia, the Forest of Elves, the Blue Moon celebration was coming to an end. We all waved goodbye as the Blue Moon Goddess stepped on a light blue cloud and floated away. It was breathtaking to watch.

With the celebration was over, everyone began the task of cleaning up. I tried to help, but the elves insisted that I was a guest. Even though I no longer had any pain, they insisted I take it easy.

I leaned over to Nessa. "Nessa, if you don't need me down here, I would really like to go lay down. After that big wonderful meal and celebration, I am very tired and would like to rest."

Nessa agreed. "I know you say your pain has eased since Glitz gave you some of our elf tears to heal your wound, but you are still not at your best."

She and another elf walked with me to my room. We got into the cage lift. Nessa and the other elf pulled the ropes to bring us up to my room.

As we ascended, I admired how beautiful everything was in Elfinnia. In the glow of the evening, I could see some of the elves going up and down in cage lifts while others climbed the stairs that spiraled around the big trees.

Some of the younger elves were climbing the trees like cats. Some flew on huge hawks and others chatted into the night.

I noticed a great waterfall in the distance. Looking at it gave me an idea of how high up we were. Everything was made easier to see in the night because of the thousands and thousands of lightning bugs that lit up the forest.

There were many visiting fairies that had come for the celebration. Perhaps Glitz had found a friend to talk to. This whole place was so amazing to see, I couldn't wait to get to my room and write in my adventure journal. *This place is like I dream* I thought to myself.

Once we arrived and Nessa helped me get ready and comfortably settled in bed, I asked her if they were able to save anything from our wagon.

She brought me my mother's old bag that held my journal and other items. She also brought my mother's old guitar.

"Oh thank God! I had hoped and prayed my mother's guitar had not been destroyed. It's a little singed in some places, but I think I can still play it. Thank you."

I began to strum and tune the instrument.

"Wow, you are really good," said Nessa. "Maybe before you leave on your journey you can play with our musical elves and fairies."

"I would love to," I replied.

Nessa then pulled my journal out of my mother's bag. "What sort of things have you written in your journal so far? I would love to read it." She dusted the journal off and handed it to me.

"Well, so far I have written my reasons for making this journey. I've written about meeting Glitz and how we helped Father create the Labyrinth Garden and how I met Phoebe, Deena and Sky. I also wrote about the hobbits and all that happened there and how nice they all were to us." I flipped the pages to show Nessa my illustrations.

"You are very talented," said the other elf as she looked on from behind us.

"Thank you," I said smiling.

"If you don't mind, Evanwood wanted me to check your wound one last time before you went to sleep," Nessa said.

She carefully took off the bandages. "I cannot believe this! It doesn't look like an arrow puncture but rather like a bruise."

"It's because of the elf tears, Nessa." said the other elf.

"I know, but this is the first time I have seen it work on a wound like that. I have seen the tears do many things but nothing like that. Remember Piper, I am not as old as you are." We all laughed.

"Elves are somewhat immortal beings," Nessa explained. "We do age, but at a much, much slower pace than humans. What looks like a young teenage elf to you is probably about 140 years old. An elf that looks middle-aged, like Piper, is probably around 375 years old."

"Wow!" I said. "That means you and Piper have really seen a lot of changes. In some ways you are like vampires. They can live forever."

"Yes, in a way, but we can live in the sunlight and vampires can't. We sleep at night. Well some of us do anyway. I am more of what you might call a night owl," said Nessa.

"Okay, now it's getting very late, and our guest needs her sleep," Evanwood said coming up the spiral staircase. "You need your rest, so don't stay up too late writing and drawing. You and your friends have hard training ahead if you want to learn how to protect yourselves. Rest, and we'll see you in the morning."

When they left the room, I started writing in my journal. I wrote about saving the stubborn owl, Cozmo. I hope wherever he is now that he is okay. Being a golden owl and with his luck, he most likely has been captured again. However, I had a feeling I hadn't seen the last of him.

I drew pictures of him, first at the troll's campsite, then flying away. I also wrote about being struck by the poison arrow from the Dark Elf.

I tried to describe the beauty of Elfinnia through my writings and drawings, but I doubt I did it justice. This place is breathtakingly beautiful. I would love to come back here with my father some day. I wondered if he and my mother had ever visited such a place.

It was late, and I knew I need to rest. Tomorrow would be a busy day.

The next morning I awakened to a gorgeous day. A breakfast of exotic fruits and some type of egg with juice was waiting by my bed.

There was a note too. It read that once I was finished with breakfast, I would find an outfit in the closet that should fit so I could start my training. Everyone was waiting outside, so I quickly ate and changed.

I walked down the spiral staircase and was pointed to nearby open field where the others were already gathered.

A few of the elves and fairies were showing Glitz how to use what look like tiny glass balls that burst when they hit the ground. Sky was running in and out through the trees and changing his fur to blend in with the forest. The elves were showing him how to change his pattern faster than he'd ever been able to.

Deena was learning how to use her horn as a sword. While she was fighting, she leaped into the air—wings came out from her sides and she was flying. She seemed as stunned as the rest of us.

She flew around us a few times before finally landing. I ran toward her.

"How did you do that? I did not know unicorns had wings. I thought only Pegasus were able to fly."

"I think that is my doing," said Evanwood. "During the celebration and feast I gave Deena an elixir of Pegasus blood to drink. I did not realize it would work so quickly, but I'm pleased that it did."

"Did it hurt?" I asked Deena.

"A little, but I like the results. This could really come in handy," she said with a huge smile on her face.

"Man, I wish I could have wings," said Sky running towards us. "Do you have any more of that elixir, Evan?"

I laughed. "Now you would look silly with wings, Sky. You already have amazing abilities."

"Amazing they may be, but I still think it would be cool. Don't you? Wouldn't you love to be able to fly like that Murry?"

I thought for a minute and nodded. "It would be kind of neat. I wonder Evan, would people who are not pure of heart still see her as a normal horse or would they now see her for who she really is, a unicorn?"

"Don't worry about that my child, only the pure of heart and magical creatures can still see her true form," he explained.

Evanwood led me to the field to start my training. I began with wooden swords, learning how to defend myself. Then I learned how to shoot with a bow and arrow. That was fun!

With all the training I had done with my father, I never learned how to use a bow and arrow. We did that next. It was a little difficult at first because of my shoulder, but after a few days of practice, I began to get the hang of it. Nessa even said I shoot like an elf.

On our last evening in Elfinnia, we all gathered together for dinner. While we were eating, I heard a rustling sound coming from the nearby bushes. I could see that the elves were all on edge. "What is wrong, Nessa?"

"Someone is coming, and it's not an elf," she said as she walked closer to where the sound was coming from.

"I didn't know elves could sense other elves," I said.

"It's one of our gifts," she explained.

She signaled me to be quiet and quickly grabbed what was behind the bushes.

"Who are you and what business do you have here?"

"I am looking for someone named Murranda. I am a friend of Phoebe's. She has a message for her," said the small girl.

"I am Murranda," I said, approaching her with some caution. "What is your name, little one?"

"I am Phoenix," she said. "This is for you."

She handed me a note.

My Dear Murry,

If you get this I will know you are okay. In fact, if you will hold the necklace Phoenix is wearing, I will know for sure.

As I read, Phoenix handed me the necklace. I held it in my hands and continued:

Remember the roses you gave first to your father and then to me? Well, we have been watching you and have seen the things you've been going through. We know that you were shot with an arrow. When your father saw this, he and another man got into a carriage to come look for you. I have found a way to guide him to me. I will try to convince them to stay here so you can continue on your journey in peace. I know at the moment you are safe. If you should face true danger again, I'll help them find you.

Unfortunately, I know why this is happening to you. I cannot go into details, but you should know that it's the work of the Sorceress and the Dark Prince. I don't think they want you dead, they just want YOU and your necklace and ring.

I am very happy that you are in the forest of elves. They are my friends. Knowing them, I'm sure they are training you and your friends for the great battle you will be facing one day. But, take heart. I see that you will not be alone or out-numbered. You and your friends will meet others who will stand by you and fight alongside you.

I prayed that you and your friends wouldn't have to face this evil as you journeyed in search of this thing you must find, but I see that you will. Before you face the ultimate battle, you will have some small battles to face. So please pay close attention to what my elf friends have to teach you. Some of those you will face in small battles will turn out to be your best allies.

Until we meet again, allow my friend Phoenix to join you on your journey. She will be of great help when needed.

I will keep your father and his friend here with me as long as I can. Take care, and know I am always with you.

Phoebe.

Oh my poor father, I thought. I do hope Phoebe is able to find a way to get him to come to her. I know he means well, but I want to do this on my own. It's something I must do on my own."

"You are not on your own, Murry," Glitz said, as he flew to me and grew to his boyish size. "You forget we are on this journey with you."

"I know you are. I just meant as far as my father was concerned. If you don't mind, please get out of my head and stop reading my thoughts or just don't let me know you are reading them." I said sarcastically.

His face reddened. He lowered his head, shrunk back to his fairy size and flew behind Deena. I couldn't help but shake my head and laugh.

I rubbed the tiger's eye as I held the necklace. "I wonder if Phoebe can hear me as I hold this?"

"You could try, ma'am," replied Phoenix. "She seems to know her magic. She told me that if I got lost on my way to find you, I should hold the necklace tightly and she would be with me."

I held the tiger's eye necklace with both hands. "Phoebe, I hope you can hear me. PLEASE find a way to get my father and Jeffery to you. Don't let them come looking for me. I am okay. In fact, I am starting my defensive training with the elves now. If I need help, I will find a way to let all of you know. I will let your friend Phoenix join us on the journey."

I handed the necklace back to Phoenix and thanked her for bringing the message to me. "Will you join me on my journey?" I asked.

"Yes, ma'am I will, but only for a while. I am also on a journey looking for my family. My parents died when I was a baby. An elderly lady raised me as long as she was able, then she gave me to the gypsies. That is how I met your friend. However, I know I have other family members out there somewhere. I have to try and find them."

"Well then, it's settled. You will join us. Maybe you should join us for the defensive training."

"I will be okay as far as that goes, Ma'am. I am fast and cunning, and I'm getting faster and more cunning by the day."

Nessa walked over to where Evanwood stood. "Do you sense there is something different about this Phoenix girl?"

"Now that you mention it, I do. I don't think she's fully mortal. I get the feeling there is something mystical about her. I cannot tell if it's good or evil, but I think you and Jett may need to see about joining Murry on this journey so you can keep an eye on Phoenix."

Nessa looked at Evanwood. "I am not sure Jett wants to join them. You know how he feels about Murry." She looked around for her brother.

"Don't worry about him. I will convince him to join you all. You just get her to allow you to go along."

"What about you, Evan? We may need your knowledge and magic." Nessa grabbed his hands with desperation in her eyes.

"You will be fine, sister. I have taught you all that I know. Just wear this necklace and if you need anything just find some water and stick the necklace in it, or insert it into the ground and ask for me, and I will appear." Evanwood handed her a necklace with a light blue crystal.

Nessa put on the necklace and walked over to where we were training. She grabbed my arm and led me away from Phoenix.

"What is wrong?" I asked.

"We need to talk about your journey and your new friend," she said. "My brother Evan and I think there is something about Phoenix—you need to be wary of her."

"What is it? What are you talking about? Phoebe says she is a friend of hers and if Phoebe can trust her, so can I."

"Murry, I don't think she is what she appears to be. I don't know what she is, but Evan and I feel that she is not mortal. There is something mystical about her. We don't know if it's good or evil, but we do know you need to be careful around her. If you insist on letting her join you on your quest, then I beg you to let Jett and I go with you, too."

"Jett? But he does not trust me."

"Don't worry about my brother. Evan is talking to him. He will convince Jett that it would be best for us to join you. We are the best warriors here, and you will need all the help you can get.

"Maybe you are right about needing more protection. Yes, you can join us. Even though I have had all this training, and I can tell I am getting better, my confidence is not where it should be. I would like it if you came as my protectors." We walked back to join the group.

I didn't feel the same way as Nessa and Evan felt about Phoenix. She is merely a child and seemed harmless. As far as I was concerned, if she was a friend of Phoebe's, and Phoebe thought it best I bring her with me, then I would. I have complete trust in Phoebe.

I gathered everyone around and readied the group to leave. I needed to continue my search. We no longer had a wagon, so we would leave on foot. The other elves made us backpacks out of strong leaves and bamboo. They also made some satchels that would fit over the backs of Deena and Sky.

These items made it possible for us to carry the weapons that we might need as well as supplies.

"Evan, I want to thank you for all your help," I said. I noticed a potted plant on the gathering table with one of my Murry Roses.

I looked over and saw Glitz smiling. He said, "Something told me you were going to give Evanwood one of your roses, so I thought I would go ahead and have it ready before we left."

"Were you getting in my head again Glitz?"

"No, I just know you. This way if we get into any trouble, Evan will have a way to find us. Elves can get places faster than humans," he explained.

"Well Evan, now that you have the rose it's time for us to leave. I will miss you all, but I truly believe we will meet again soon." I waved goodbye and hopped on Deena's back.

Where to next? I thought to myself as we walked on the nearby trail. *Away from Elfinnia.*

We walked for miles with everyone telling stories of their adventures. I happened to look down at the trail and noticed something red and shiny.

"WAIT!" I yelled. I hopped off of Deena and bent down to pick up one of the shiny items. It was a trail of tiny rubies going in the direction of the Shadow Land.

"Deena," I cried, "I think I have found our wounded, obnoxious friend Cozmo, And I believe he is still hurt and bleeding."

"Really," said Deena. "I am shocked he has not yet been captured. Maybe his Irish luck hasn't run out yet," she laughed.

"Well whether it has or hasn't, I think we need to look for him before he does get himself in trouble," I said.

"You have got to be kidding me. That ugly, flying, golden statue is the least of our worries. If we go the way you are suggesting, we'll be entering the Shadow Land," Glitz butted in. "Remember the Dark Elf, the Prince…the Sorceress."

"If Murry wants to find this owl, now would be the time to do it. For the next three days everyone will be safe in the Shadow Land," Jett said. "It's the weekend of the Masquerade Ball and the only time of peace."

"My brother is right," added Nessa. "The Masquerade Ball happens once a year. It came about when the two sisters left each other, and the Dark Prince and the King agreed to grant one weekend a year as a time for the two sisters to reunite. Those of us in this realm are allowed to join in the celebration. Humans call this time Halloween or All Hallows Eve."

"Talk about your ultimate haunted house," I said. "Glitz, do you remember Phoebe said about how I will have to visit the Shadow Land to save someone or to find something I needed? Maybe this is what she was talking about. Maybe I am supposed to go in and rescue Cozmo from whatever is in there."

"I don't know, Murry," Glitz said in a worried voice. "I really don't think we should go in there even if it's the weekend of peace. You cannot trust the creatures that live there. They are evil. When have they ever followed the rules?"

I looked at everyone and then looked toward the Shadow Land. I put both hands around the charm of the necklace Phoebe gave me, and then I looked back at the group.

"I have to trust my instincts and go after the owl. You can either come with me, or you can stay here and wait for me. But, I am going."

"Wait, Murry!" Nessa said. "If you are going, so am I."

"Same here," said Sky.

"Me too," said Jett.

"I am not going to let you have all the fun. I too am coming," said Phoenix.

"Well, I promised your mother that unicorns would always be there for her and her family, so I am in too."

I turned and looked at Glitz. "Don't think I'm going to let you leave me out here holding the bags. If you all are going, so am I," he said with a nervous, high-pitched voice. "I'm not s-s-scared. This is the weekend of peace, so we all should be fine."

I did not know if this was the right thing to do, but something in my gut told me it was. We continued walking into the forest. I held on to my necklace hoping that it would warn me of approaching danger.

I had no idea what we would face, but I knew that being in the Shadow Land brought us closer to the Dark Elf. He had already injured me once. I couldn't help but wonder if entering the Shadow Land and possibly meeting the Sorceress and The Dark Prince would bring me closer to finding whatever I was looking for. Or, perhaps an important clue would be revealed to me. One thing I was certain of was that this weekend should prove to be very interesting.

CHAPTER 10

Back at the Gypsy Fair, Phoebe was in her carriage house preparing for the arrival of Murranda's father and his servant Jeffery, when there was a knock on her door.

Another older gypsy lady opened the door. "Phoebe, are you in here? There are two well-dressed strangers in a horse and buggy asking about your friends."

"Yes, Sheila, I am in the back. I will be out soon."

"What was that you said about my friends?" asked Phoebe.

"There are two men asking about them. I came here to warn you. The gypsies are frightened they telling the men to leave."

"Send them to me Sheila. I have been expecting them. The man is Murry's father," said Phoebe.

"Her father? We did not know. Follow me and I will take you to them."

Sheila led Phoebe to meet them before the others could send them off. When they arrived, Rudy and Jeffery were asking the other gypsies about Murranda and her friends. Rudy looked up at Phoebe and couldn't help but stare at her for a moment.

"I am sorry for staring, but do I know you?" he asked.

"Hello Rudy, old friend. It's me, Phoebe."

"Phoebe. Yes, I do remember now. Last time I saw you was... "

"Before the death of Morinda," Phoebe interrupted. "I am guessing you are here looking for your daughter," she said looking over at Jeffery.

"I too remember you," said Jeffery, scratching his head. "The last time I saw you, my lady, you had just left your sister at the Shadow Land and were living with the elves in Elfinnia."

"Yes, old friend. I was getting ready to return to the Shadow Land for the weekend of peace."

"So, have you seen my daughter Murranda?" Rudy interrupted. As he spoke, he noticed the Murry Rose on Phoebe's window ledge.

"You have seen her! You have one of Murranda's special roses, just like this one!"

He grabbed his rose out of the carriage to show her. "You have to help us find her! She is in a lot of trouble. I saw her get struck by an arrow. She's injured and needs me."

Rudy began pacing back and forth.

"Calm down Rudy, old friend," said Phoebe, grabbing his shoulder.

"Calm down? How can I? You remember what happened between my wife, your sister and the Dark Prince the last time. Now I'm allowing my child to face the same thing. She has no idea what she's up against. Don't you remember the last thing the Prince said about my family?" Rudy finally sat down on an old log, trying to collect his thoughts.

"Yes, I remember everything. Your daughter was here, but she left with her guardians, and she is doing fine. My elf friends and her fairy friend, Glitz, have healed her. I know this is difficult for you, but this journey Murry is on is one she has to make, and she has to do it without your help. This is no different than when you and your wife, or you and Jeffrey made all those journeys in the past."

"But this is different, Phoebe. This time it's MY ONLY daughter. I am not going to just sit here and do nothing. You said she is in the Elvinnia so that is where I am going now. Come on, Jeffery. We have a ride ahead of us. We must continue."

"Wait Rudy!" called Phoebe. "The two of you have been on the road for days. You need to rest, and I can see you did not pack enough supplies. So I must insist that you stay at least one night and have some food and get some rest. Your horses need it as well. Your daughter is still with my friends, so you have time."

Phoebe led Rudy and Jeffery to her home and signaled for the gypsies to take care of their horses for the night.

As she prepared dinner, Rudy and Jeffery sat on her couches trying to relax. Rudy was still feeling very uneasy about not continuing his search.

"I cannot just sit here while my daughter is somewhere out there in danger. I promised my wife on her deathbed that I would always keep our daughter safe, and what do I do? I let her go on this crazy journey and get hurt. Thank you, Phoebe for your hospitality, but I need to look for her. How can I be sure she has not left the elf forest and maybe wondered into the Shadow Land?"

"You have to trust me on this, old friend, and trust your daughter. We must continue to watch the rose. She will be just fine. Do you remember the necklace I once gave your wife?"

"Yes, I do. It helped us through a lot of our journey. We never did find out what the ring was for, or at least I did not. There was one night when my wife was alone somewhere with the Dark Prince. That was a night I will never forget. It still haunts me to this day, and now because of me, my daughter may have to face the same nightmare."

"Sir, remember what we talked about before. You have to trust her, and I think what Phoebe is trying to say is that she gave Murry something like the necklace your wife had," explained Jeffrey.

"Not something like the necklace, but the necklace and ring itself. Didn't you notice when you were safely home that the necklace and ring were gone."

"Yes, but my wife and I thought we had lost them with some of our supplies during our last encounter with your sister," Rudy said, shrugging his shoulders.

"No. When the journey was over, the ring and necklace came back to me. That let me know that you were safe, and you had fulfilled what you set out to do. If only one of the items had come back to me it would have meant that your journey had ended and that one or both of you had died." Phoebe said looking down.

"Wow, Phoebe! Thanks for making me feel so much better!" Rudy said sarcastically.

"But Sir, as you can see, neither item has come back here," said Jeffery.

As the two men were talking, Phoebe grabbed some bowls and poured some stew into both of them. While she had her back to them, she took a small bottle from the spice rack and poured it into the bowls. *This should keep them here so that Murranda can continue her journey on her own. I am sorry old friends, but this is how it must be.*

She turned and handed the bowls to Rudy and Jeffery.

"Here, I am sure the two of you are hungry. Eat and rest. Your horses are eating and resting and so should you both. You can leave at sunrise."

"Okay Phoebe. We will stay the night. One night and then we leave to look for them in the morning," said Rudy as he began eating.

"I have to say, my lady, this is some fine stew," Jeffery said, tipping his hand to Phoebe.

"Let's just say it's a family recipe. It will warm your bones and get you ready for a good night of sleep," explained Phoebe.

When they had finished dinner, Rudy and Jeffery started to feel very sleepy.

"You are right about making us feel relaxed and ready for bed. I think I'll just lay right here," said Rudy, yawning and stretching out on the couch.

"Well you are more than welcome to make yourself at home," Phoebe said.

"Jeffery, you can use this chair. It will lay back so you can rest." As soon as she sat Jeffery on the chair the two men were out like a light.

After they fell asleep Sheila came knocking again. "Hey Phoebe, I had to stop. I could smell your family's famous stew as I walked past. You wouldn't have any more of that would you?" she asked.

"Shhhh!" Phoebe said pressing her finger to her lips. "Yes, you can have some as long as you stay here and watch over my friends as they sleep. They will be sleeping for days. In fact, I am hoping they will stay asleep for a week." She handed Sheila a jar filled with gravy from the stew.

"Just make sure they drink some of this gravy once a day. They will sleep, but their minds will know what to do. I have to go to the Shadow Land. It's getting to be that time. I hope to return before they wake up."

"But what if they wake up before you return? What do I do then?" asked Sheila.

"They will be upset. Here," she said handing Sheila two pieces of paper, "have them read this and they will understand. Don't stop them if they want to leave. In fact, help them get ready. I will return soon."

Phoebe kissed her friend on the cheek and left for the Shadow Land. Phoebe had a feeling that this weekend might be the last time she would see her sister. Murranda's visit would change everything in the Shadow Land and in Xeenoephillia. Part of her was sad about it, but at the same time, she knew that the greater good had to happen.

Phoebe though about how Murry's father would react once he and Jeffery woke from their sleep. Hopefully, someday Rudy would understand why it was necessary. She couldn't worry about that now. Murry needed to find her own way and fulfill her destiny and she would need all the help Phoebe could provide.

CHAPTER 11

𝓜y friends and I had arrived at the entrance to the Shadow Land. We were hoping to find Cozmo.

"Everything is so dark and foggy here," I said, cautious to walk very close to Deena. I held tightly to the sword attached to my belt.

"Don't worry Murry. As we said before, this is the weekend of peace. Everyone here is most likely getting ready for the festivities," Nessa explained.

She put her hand on my shoulder as if to tell me to let go of my sword. So I did. As we entered the dark, we could hear strange sounds coming from all directions. Each time we heard them Glitz and I jumped. The others tried to calm us. Then I heard a familiar voice coming from a nearby tree.

"How did that little girl think she was going to take care of someone like me when she couldn't even tie a proper bandage? Now look at me. I have blood everywhere, and with the blood dripping and turning into stupid rubies, I am just leading every poor, stupid, greedy human my way."

"Did you guys hear that?" I asked. "I think it's Cozmo! He's somewhere close."

"Are you sure we need to find and help that brainless doorstopper?" Deena asked as she tried to walk away from the sound.

"Deena, we all agreed to do this, to help him no matter how obnoxious he is. We just have to follow that sound and find him before someone else does."

I pointed in the direction of his voice. Suddenly, two arrows attached to a net flew by. It wrapped itself around the wounded owl which had been perched above us in a tree. He was whisked away before we could do anything."

"Oh no we are too late." I cried.

"What was that and where is it taking Cozmo?" asked Glitz.

"From the look of those arrows, I'd say it was another Dark Elf," noted Jett. He climbed up the tree where Cozmo had been and examined the marks the arrows left. "If that is that case, he is most likely being taken to the Dark Castle of the Sorceress and the Prince."

"But I thought this weekend was of peace. Why did they capture him?"

"I am not sure Murry, but if we are going to help your feathered friend we need to follow the direction of the arrows." Nessa said as she led the group.

"What if it's a trap?" Glitz asked, frightened. "I knew we should not have come here. Nothing good ever happens in the Shadow Land."

"I understand you are scared Glitz. I am too," I said as I put my arm around him.

Glitz shook his head, stood up straight and said, "I-I-I'm not sc-sc-scared. I am just concerned about you, Murry. I promised your father I would watch over you, that's all."

"And you are doing a great job," I said, "but we need to find Cozmo."

"Well, if we are going to find your friend we need to go now while the trail is still fresh," said Jett. "Once we find the owl, I am sure we can find out what is going on."

We followed Jett from the ground as he climbed up the tall trees following the cuts in the trees left by the arrows.

"It looks as though the arrow is enchanted," Nessa pointed out. "Normally, arrows only go one way, straight, or they may slightly turn if the arrow is curved, but this arrow went in so many directions, left, right, up high then low then high again. This is definitely the work of the Dark Elf."

As we continued following, I couldn't believe all the strange creatures I was seeing in the Shadow Land. Some had human bodies but skin like lizards. Some looked like panthers and tigers. There were even those that appeared to be lycans—half wolf, half human creatures that changed back and forth in the darkness of the forest.

There were also regular wolves and large birds such as hawks and buzzards, as well as shadow-like people. I couldn't tell if they were real or just shadows of other things lurking, but there were no other humans.

They were not bothering us and most of them seemed not to notice we were here. Those that did simply passed us by. They were all moving in the same direction as we were.

"Deena, do you know what these shadows are?" I asked.

"Yes, Murry. They protect the entrance to the Shadow Land. They don't want people from our realm to see what lies here. They can transform themselves into any shape yet remain their black or dark gray color. There have even been cases where some of them have transformed into other people. They are shapes-shifters."

I grew frightened. "They are not here to hurt us," Deena said, "If they are going this way, then the netted arrows that took Cozmo must be taking him to the Dark Castle and the Sorceress, I wonder if she knows we are here."

"How would they know we are here, and why would she care?" I asked.

"Remember Phoebe's letter, Murry?" Glitz asked. "She said that her sister, the Sorceress, is after your necklace and ring. Maybe she can sense that they are near."

We continued following the arrow's path toward the Dark Castle. I looked around at all the different sites and was not watching where I was going.

I bumped into someone, looking up I realized it was a lycan. Two more flanked our group.

"Watch where you are going human!" one yelled. "Why do we allow these humans to come into our land so freely? They are nothing more than a snack."

"We all agreed to the terms of the law that on the weekend of All-Hallows Eve, there would be peace between the two lands," a female lycan snapped.

"I never agreed to any peace signing. No one asked me. The only good human is a dead human," said the male, licking his lips.

I was not feeling very safe. I gripped my sword.

"We are wild! We follow what we choose! Law means nothing to us! Why should we obey a Vampire Prince that wants to invite these kind here. They turn us into circus freaks for you humans to stare at…"

"You have to excuse my mate. He is not very fond of strangers," explained the female.

"I can tell. We are just here to find our owl friend, maybe you've seen him?" said Sky, stepping between me and the lycans.

"My name is Lana, and this is Bane. And you are?" the female asked.

"My name is Murranda." I said. Lana couldn't stop staring at me.

"I am so sorry for staring, but I have seen you before," she said.

"She is no one you know," Deena said nudging me away from the lycans.

"Ahh Unicorn—I remember you," said Bane, grinning a toothy grin. "How long has it been since we crossed paths? Well at least this time it's under better circumstances."

"Not long enough in my opinion."

"I agree," said Lana growling at Bane, "but unlike my mate, I intend to obey the laws here. And, if I have anything to say about it, so will he."

"You cannot tell me what to do. I am the male around here," Bane snarled, puffing up his chest.

"You may be the male, but who is the alpha in our pack?" Lana snarled back, pushing Bane hard enough to knock him over. "Don't forget whose daughter I am."

"Oh, so you are going to continue to hold that over my head." Bane said. He retreated somewhat, pretending to lick wounds.

"Excuse him," explained Lana. "He tends to show more bark than bite. Your owl friend…we've seen him. The Dark Elf took him away and I think we may know why. They most likely will use him as the trophy for the annual games. Your friend is a golden owl after all. Come, we will show you."

Bane and Lana transformed themselves into wolves—him into a silver hair and her, pure white. Despite our reservations, we followed them through the woods.

We approached the walls of the Dark Castle and got as close as we could. In the top of the castle's tower was the netted arrow. Cozmo was flapping around inside.

We noticed other people and creatures heading towards the castle. Some were riding on horseback while others were in carriages. We saw some flying on dragons, and on Pegasus. We also saw centaurs, fawns and giants on foot. We turned to see the royal carriage with the King and Queen. The closer we got to the castle, the more crowded it became.

Suddenly we heard a giant call out. "Hey there! Would you like a lift? I would hate to step on you and your friends by accident." He held out his hand.

"Thank you very much. That would be nice of you." I said as my friends and I climbed onto his palm.

"You look familiar to me. Morinda is that you? You haven't aged a bit for a mortal. It's me, Kandor," he said.

"Nice to meet you Kandor. I am sorry to disappoint you, but I am not Morinda. I am Murranda. Morinda was my mother."

"Oh, I am sorry. You look so much like your her. How is she and your father Rudy?"

"My father is well," I said. "But my mother is dead—during my birth."

When I told Kandor what had happened to my mother, he looked very sad. "I am sorry to hear about your mother. Is your father with you? Is he already inside the castle waiting for you?"

I shook my head, no. Then he stopped and turned about to go the other way.

"WAIT! What are you doing? I need to get to the castle. Why are you turning around?"

"I don't think it's safe for you to be here, child. This is not a place for you," he said.

"But, this is the weekend of peace. I will be fine. Please put us down. We will walk the rest of the way ourselves."

"Please, Kandor, she is right. We must go in," Deena said.

Kandor stopped and looked closely at Deena. "Don't I know you?"

"Yes you do know me. We don't have a lot of time. Please my friend, take us into the castle. We will be fine. I promise."

Kandor did just that. When we were inside the gates, Kandor let down his hand so we could step off.

"Thank you for your help. We'll be ok from here," I said.

"If you get in trouble, find Kandor. I will help you," he said.

The castle was huge. There was so much beauty in this place, but I could feel the evil it held. The architecture and the artwork were breathtaking. There was magic in this place. Everything felt both so alive but carried the chill of death. Ghosts floated in and out of walls.

I was looking around at all the artwork and was so taken, I bumped into someone again. Thinking it was Jett, I looked up to excuse myself. Instead I was face to face with a man I had never seen.

He was exceeding handsome, tall well-built, and well-dressed, with very dark almost black hair down to his shoulders, pale skin and dark eyes that seemed to have specks of gold in them. When I looked into his eyes, I found it difficult to speak.

I could only stammer out an apology "I…I…I." Deena bumped me to stop me from embarrassing myself even more. "I'm sorry I was not looking where I was going," I finally said.

"That is fine," he replied. "In fact it was my pleasure bumping into you again Morinda. You haven't changed a bit. Is your husband Rudolpho here with you?"

As he talked I turned my head away. For some reason I felt shy around him. Deena looked as if she wanted to either attack him or just pull me away from him. She stomped her hooves against the ground. I could tell that she did not like this man.

"I am sorry sir, but you are mistaken. I am not Morinda, I am her daughter, Murranda."

The gentleman laughed, "Something told me you were not her, but I had to ask. You look so much like your mother. Allow me to introduce myself. I am Prince Demitri Santiago."

He took my right hand and kissed the back of it ever so gently. I could feel his cold breath on my skin and one of his fangs brush against the back of my hand.

His hand turned cold and deathlike in mine, I yanked my hand away and gasped, "You are the Dark Prince!"

"You and your friends must be here for the Grand Masquerade Ball and Festival," he said, not even flinching at my reactions.

"Yes, we are here for that and also to look for a friend of ours who seems to have been captured by one of your dark elves…a golden owl named Cozmo. Perhaps you've seen him?"

"One of my people captured someone during the weekend of peace? I will find out who it was and why. If your friend is truly a golden owl, then maybe my dark elves mistook him for a trophy," he said slyly. "However, since he is your friend, I will make sure they return him to you. Until I can find him, please enjoy everything here. My castle is your castle."

He turned to walk away, but stopped short, looking back at us, "would you do me the honor of joining me for dinner?"

"I would like that," I said, slightly nervous. "You said you knew my mother and met my father, I would like to hear more about that"

I saw the worried expression in Deena's eye as soon as I said it. I looked over at Glitz and Sky and they didn't know what to say either.

Sky finally broke the tension. "Well, if you would be so kind as to point us to our rooms, we would be very appreciative."

"Oh, but of course. Jezzica!" he called out.

From seemingly nowhere, a dark but pale-skinned figure emerged from the shadows. She wore a blood-red dress with a black web-like cape draped across the back. I immediately sensed she was also a vampire

Demitri extended his hand in our direction, "can you show our special guests to their suites? They will be staying on the same level as the King and Queen."

"Yes, my Prince," she said, nodding in acknowledgement.

Jezzica led us down the hallway. Floating candles lined the walls, showing us the way down the hall. When I looked behind me, I could see them go out one by one. At the end of the hall, we stopped just short of a huge hole in the floor.

I could see people on the other side of the hallway. The hole reached from top to bottom. We could see the edge of every hallway above and below and they all met up the same way.

"Jezzica, where do we go from here?" Glitz asked. "I can fly up to the different floors but what about the others?"

"If you all form a circle around me, I will show you how to get to your proper floor and room."

Once we formed the circle, Jezzica opened up her hands with her palms facing down. A black fog formed around us trailing under our feet and lifting us toward the top of the castle. As I rose higher and higher, I looked down and saw others being led to their rooms the same ways. The guides were leading the way. Each one touched the person in front of them and they would float upwards or through the walls.

When we arrived at our rooms, Jezzica pointed out who was staying where and showed us the connector doors between the rooms.

When she opened the doors to our rooms, I couldn't believe my eyes. Each room was designed to mirror our homeland. Deena's room was forest-like as was Jett's and Nessa's. Sky's room looked like a jungle. You could hear the exotic birds and monkeys. Glitz's room looked like the rainforest, and my room looked almost exactly like my room at home.

"How did you do all of this?" I said in amazement.

"Thank the sorceress," Jezzica said, nodding her head. "If you need anything, all you have to do is pull the velvet cord and one of us will be happy to help you. Dinner will be ready in about 2 hours. Someone will come and escort you to the dining hall. You have some clothes laid out for you to wear to dinner. We all dress up for dinner here. I'm certain you will find everything to your liking."

I looked around my room and began to feel homesick. I thought of my father. I pray he is okay.

I walked over to my bed and saw the most beautiful dress I had ever seen. It was similar to Jezzica's clothing—blood red velvet and silk with black webbing draped over it. Matching gems with sewn along the outside. On the table there was a matching headpiece. I picked up the dress to get a better look.

I stood in front of the full-length mirror and put the dress next to me to see how I would look in it. The top was form fitting and the bottom part was very full. Then I noticed that the necklace and ring Phoebe gave me were a perfect match.

Someone knocked on my door. "Come in," I said. It was Jezzica.

"May I help you with your dress? As you can see it needs to be tied in the back,"

"Yes, thank you," I said, handing her the dress. "Can you give me a moment to freshen up?"

"Yes, ma'am. I will have everything you need ready when you come out."

When I returned, Jezzica was next to the vanity setting out some makeup and brushes. When she finished, she held out the dress for me to step into. She helped pull it up tied the back so tightly that I felt like I could hardly breath.

I sat on the stool in front of the vanity as she brushed my hair and applied my makeup. When she was finished, I looked in the mirror and all I could see was my mother staring back at me. I was admiring how pretty I looked, when I noticed that Jezzica had no reflection in the mirror. I jumped back from the vanity, startled.

"Is everything ok?" she asked

"You have no reflection."

"Oh that it's because I haven't fed yet. I can fix that," she continued.

I prepared to run, but she stopped me. "Don't worry, ma'am, I will not feed on you. You and your friends are all safe. I have what I need right here."

At that moment, a woman came through the door. Jezzica led her to the vanity and the woman held out her wrist.

Jezzica looked deep into the woman's eyes then softly grabbed her wrist and bit down. The woman did not flinch. In fact she seemed to enjoy it, as if it aroused her. I stood fearful, but intrigued by it all at the same time. As soon as Jezzica fed, her reflection appeared in the mirror.

"As you see, we can be more like humans once we feed," she said. "Now that you are ready, I will let you go as we get things prepared for the feast, and I think your fairy friend wants to come in."

As soon as she said that, there was a knock on the adjoining door to Glitz's room. "Come in Glitz," I said. Once he entered, the lady and Jezzica vanished.

"Now that was some exit." I said with a smile.

"What was some exit, Murry?" Glitz asked.

"Nevermind. It does not matter."

"I am not sure about all of this," Glitz said "I don't think we need to be here. I doubt that whatever it's you are searching for is in here. We just need to find Cozmo and the others and leave."

"I want to find out what the prince knows about my mother and father."

Then I began thinking; *why hasn't Father mentioned meeting the Dark Prince? Is this the reason I had to come on this journey? Is there something else that has been hidden from me? Is there something I need to learn about my mother?* I know the answers to these questions are here somewhere, and I intend to find them no matter how much danger may be involved.

12

CHAPTER 12

Glitz looked at me. "I know this is the weekend of peace. I have been to the sister's reunion before, but something is different. I can't shake this feeling Murry. Are you still wearing the necklace Phoebe gave you? Is it telling you anything?"

"Yes, I'm wearing it, and no it's not telling me anything. So that just proves that you are getting worked up for nothing. Let's find the others and join the party. I am getting hungry."

We walked down the hallway until we reached Deena's and Sky's rooms. I knocked on the door but there was no answer.

I opened Deena's door and called out, "Deena are you here?"

The room seemed empty, so I looked around. It resembled a beautiful outdoor meadow. Instead of carpet the floor was covered in soft grass and the walls looked as if you could walk through them and into the forest.

I guess it was a way of making everyone feel more at home. I had been told that the castle was a magical, enchanted place. I kept calling out for Deena, but there was no response.

Next we walked to Sky's room hoping they were in there together. His room was also empty.

"You see! You see! I told you something was not right." Glitz said as he grabbed my arm and pulled me out of the room. "We need to find them and get out of here."

"We are NOT leaving, Glitz!"

"I know we have to find them first. Then we can get out of here," he interrupted.

"No I mean they are around here somewhere. They must be looking for Cozmo. We are staying for the party and that is that. If you feel like you need to leave, then feel free to go. I will be fine."

"Did I hear someone say he wants to leave?" a voice from behind said.

I turned to see whom it was and couldn't believe my eyes.

"Phoebe, is that you?"

The woman looked like Phoebe but her hair different hair color and style and she had a darker demeanor. She wore a robe-like dress and carried a long crystal staff.

"No, I am Pheonna. Phoebe is my twin. I am sure she must be here somewhere or is on her way. Do I know you?" Pheonna asked. "You look very much like someone I have met."

"You must be thinking of my mother, Morinda. People say I look a lot like her. My name is Murranda."

"I see. So you are the one everyone in the castle is talking about. The one that seems to have caught the eye of our prince?"

"I am sorry, but you must be mistaken. The Prince and I have only met once and very briefly," I said shaking my head in disagreement.

"That may be true, but it could have something to do with your mother and the fact that you look so much like her. At one time, he had eyes for her, I think," she said. She put her hand under my chin and looked into my eyes. I did not know what to say. Pheonna was looking at my necklace. I quickly pulled away and put my hand over it. It began to vibrate against my skin.

"I am sorry for staring, but that is a lovely necklace. I have seen it before. You must have gotten it from my loving sister. Please let me escort you to the banquet. Everyone is gathering there." She looked at Glitz. "Unless you've changed your mind about staying, and want to leave."

"No, we will stay," I said as I looked over at Glitz. He was shaking his head and rolling his eyes.

The three of us walked down the hall. "Have you seen a unicorn or a charma cat around here?" I asked Pheonna.

"Your two friends, Sky and Deena. No, I have not, but I am sure they are around," she replied.

I wondered how she knew their names, but I said nothing, and we continued down the hall. We turned the corner to where the magical transporting hole was located. Then I saw a little glittery, buzzing thing flying around me, singing a song.

"Excuse me, if you will stay still, I'll be able to see what you are," I said.

Then the little fluttering thing stopped in mid air and hovered in one place like a hummingbird. It was Flutter!

"Oh, Flutter, it's you. It has been a long time. Is Dee Dee with you?" She shook her head no.

Flutter saw Glitz standing behind me and pointed her arms up in the air and feet toward the ground and grew to the same size as Glitz.

"Glitz, why don't you and Flutter go ahead and enjoy the party. Since you two can fly, you will beat us. I will be fine and will meet you down there soon."

"If you wish," said Glitz. Flutter looked back at me and signed something with her hands. Glitz looked at her and then back at me. "Flutter wants you to know that she thinks you look beautiful. The dress looks like it was made just for you."

"Thank you." I said. I had no idea she couldn't speak.

Glitz looked at me and giggled, "She speaks," Glitz said out loud. "She *is* shy, but she *chooses* not to speak much. Mainly, because not many humans know her language."

"Well maybe sometime soon you can teach me her language so I can talk to her, too." I gave Flutter a wink and a smile. "You two should go and enjoy. I will meet up with you guys soon. Both he and Flutter shrunk to their fairy size and proceeded to head down to the party.

As I walked down the hall with Pheonna, I had an uneasy feeling.

"Let me guess," Pheonna said. "You are aware of the necklace's powers and you think I am going to somehow take it from you. Let me put your mind at ease. I cannot touch the necklace while you are wearing it, and neither can the prince. Here let me show you." She reached out to grab the necklace and a bright electric light appeared and burned her hand. "You see, as long as you are wearing them no one can touch them. So, if you are ready, I can take you down. Take hold of my sleeve." As I did, she hit the floor with her staff. The top stone glowed a bloody red. In the blink of an eye we were downstairs.

The creatures and people who had come for the festival were gathered in the main hall. I saw creatures that looked human but had what appeared to be fins.

Pheonna noticed I was staring and said, "I am guessing you are wondering what those are. I suppose you've never seen a mermaid. Normally they can only walk on land during the Blue Moon, but because this lands have called a truce for this time each year, I make it possible for them to be a part of this celebration."

I looked around to see if I could find my other friends. I spotted Nessa and waved at her to come.

"Oh Murry, you look stunning."

"So do you," I said, taking a peek at what she was wearing. It reminded me of a kimono, but more woodsy with blue and green leaves.

"Have you seen Deena or Sky? I have been looking for them."

"I think they went with my brother Jett to see if they could find Cozmo."

"Are you talking about the Golden Owl?" asked Pheonna.

"Yes we are. One of your Dark Elves use a netted arrow to capture him," I replied.

"You need not worry about your golden friend. He is fine. In fact he is being treated like a king. He will be the trophy for the games we will be having here tomorrow."

"Cozmo is not a trophy! He is a living, breathing animal!" I said with a stern voice.

"We meant no harm. We all saw him in the woods and thought he would make a fine trophy."

"Is there a problem here?" A voice from behind me said. I turned and saw it was Prince Demetrius.

"No, my Prince, everything is fine," said Pheonna. "We just had a misunderstanding that is being taking care of."

"See that it is. I don't want any of my guests to be unhappy, especially when they are as exquisite as this vision of beauty." The prince said this as he lightly grabbed my gloved hand and kissed the back of it. His breath was still cold, but I was no longer scared. For some unknown reason, I still feel…shy.

"Thank you," I said. I averted my eyes from him and looked around for my friends.

I spotted Jett at the end of the hall. He was standing next to a familiar looking girl. The pair walked toward me.

The girl he was with seemed to be around my age with hair that resembled fire—it was medium length, reddish brown with gold and orange streaks and fanned behind her as she walked.

"Murry, you look beautiful for a human," Jett said with a smirk.

"Jett is right, you do. It looks as if that dress was made just for you Murry," said the girl.

"Thanks." I couldn't help but stare at the girl wondering where I had met her before.

I suppose she sensed my confusion. "It's me, Phoenix," she said as she put her hand on my shoulder.

"I couldn't believe it either," said Jett. "She seems to have aged overnight."

"I am not sure how it happened," said Phoenix.

I looked closer and noticed that her hair seemed to have feathers in it. It did not matter that she had changed. I was just so happy to see a somewhat familiar face.

"What about me?" Nessa said as she appeared behind her brother with her hand on her hips.

"You look great, too Nessa." Phoenix replied.

"Yeah, what she said," Jett repeated, "You look great."

"Back at you brother. You clean up nicely."

I looked past Jett's shoulder and just at the door, I couldn't believe my eyes. It was Wordorf and Helga Leadfoot with their kids. I excused myself from the prince and the others and ran over to them.

"It's great to see you again. How are all the other hobbits? Have there been any more problems in the village since we left?" I asked.

"Everything is fine. It's so good to see you well, my child," Wordorf said throwing his arms around me.

"Yes dear it's wonderful to see that you are safe. We have been following your adventure," Helga said. "You were very lucky to be found by the elves."

"I am fine now. In fact, I'm better than fine. The elves have taken very good care of us. If we had not been looking for our friend Cozmo, we would never have come here."

"Yes this is the only time of the year that we all put our differences aside and come together for the two sisters," said Wordorf.

"Where are your friends, Murry? We want to sit next to Glitz during dinner," the kids said.

"Glitz ran into some of his fairy friends, so he is somewhere around. As far as Sky and Deena, I was in fact looking for them, but I am sure they are around somewhere too," I said.

Hanna tugged on her mother's skirt and pointed over to where she saw Glitz, She waved to get his attention. Glitz saw the kids and motioned to them to join him and Flutter.

"Mom, can we?" The kids asked simultaneously looking up with doe-like eyes.

"Now how can anyone say no when you give us that look?" She said as she kissed both of them on the cheek. "But remember to mind your manners."

The kids raced over to the fairy table.

I excused myself from Wordorf and Helga when some of their friends came to talk to them.

I walked through the grand hall. The high ceiling in the ballroom seemed to stretch for miles. Tiny glitter specks dotted the top—it looked like stars. I wandered into another hallway that had portraits of different kings, queens, princes, and princesses.

"My family has lived here in the Shadow Land and in this castle for centuries," the Prince said.

I jumped, assuming I was alone.

"I am sorry for startling you. I saw you heading this way and I wanted to tell you that the feast is about to begin. I wanted to escort you to your seat next to me."

"That is okay," I said, lightly grabbing his arm which he had extended for me. "You may escort me to my seat. However, you must do one thing for me."

"Name it," he said.

"Prince Demitri, after dinner if it is not too much trouble, I would love a private tour through the castle. I want you to tell me things that only a few would know. Plus, I want you to tell me what you know about my family. It seems you were acquainted with my mother and father. My father has never once mentioned you in his stories, I was hoping you would tell me."

"I would love to, but only if you will stop referring to me as Prince Demetrius and just call me Demitri. I hope you will think of me as a friend. I may be a vampire, but I do have feelings. First, let's eat. I am starving."

"I did not think vampires ate. I thought they only drank blood," I said as we continued walking.

"We eat. We just prefer our meat VERY RARE. Not to disturb our guests, my chef knows to prepare my meals. Cooked on the outside and bloody in the middle," he whispered in my ear. I couldn't help but laugh.

We arrived at our table, and I noticed that the King and Queen of Xeenoephillia were seated there. Suddenly someone's hands covered my eyes. "Guess who?" said the voice.

I turned around and there stood Phoebe.

"Phoebe you are here!" I said as I hugged her. I excused myself from Demitri and led Phoebe away from the table.

"Thank you for taking care of the situation with my father and Jeffery. By the way, how are they doing?"

"Your father and Jeffery are fine. It was nice to catch up with them. I put an elixir in the stew I fed them for dinner. I have a good friend watching over them."

"Wait! You knew my father and Jeffery? How? He never mentioned you. In fact, it seems that he left a lot of things out of his stories." I said.

"I am sorry he did not tell you. I do know your father and Jeffery, and I also knew your mother," explained Phoebe.

She tried to comfort me by putting her arm around my shoulder. She was about to tell me more when a bright light appeared in the center of the ballroom, and we heard a lovely melody. There was a flash of smoke and Pheonna appeared to announce that dinner was served.

"Well, I think that is your cue to get back to your table and my cue to join my sister." Phoebe snapped her fingers, and poof, she vanished and reappeared in the center of the ballroom.

"We want to thank you for coming to our celebration," Pheonna said to all the guests. "My sister and I have always been close, and even though we choose to live in separate lands, we celebrate the fact our Prince from the Shadow Land and your King of Xeenoephillia have agreed to allow a peace to come between the two lands during our favorite time of the year, 'All Hollow's Eve'."

"What my sister is trying to say," Phoebe added, "is enjoy the feast."

"Afterwards," Pheonna announced, "there will be a tour through the castle and storytelling for the kids. Tomorrow the games will begin followed by—the Masquerade Ball."

Pheonna looked over at her sister and put her arm around her shoulder. Then she looked back at everyone in the room and said, "During this weekend of peace and celebration, please think of our castle as yours. Eat, drink, and enjoy yourselves while you are here."

When I arrived back at my table, the Prince and the King and all the men at the table stood. I walked over to the King and bowed. Because my family and the royal family had been so close for so long, I also gave him and the queen a kiss on the cheek. I hugged the prince and princess. Prince Demitri let out my seat as I sat down.

It was apparent that Pheonna was not happy I was sitting next to the prince. She glared at me and said, "I believe that this will be a weekend no one will ever forget. In fact, for some of you this weekend may be life changing."

I did not know how to react, so I remained quiet. I noticed how the Prince and some of my friends and others looked over at Pheonna. Their expressions were telling her to be quiet. Was there another secret being kept from me?

As the servants began setting out the food, I noticed how tiny the serving of food looked in front of the giants. I wondered how that would be enough to satisfy them. I could tell they were wondering the same thing by the way they were looking at their plates. Pheonna pointed her staff their way, and a beam of light shot out of the crystal to the food. In seconds the food grew to giant-size portions.

Everyone clapped and the giants began eating happily.

The food was amazing. There were things of all types to fit everyone's taste. "I cannot get over how much you look like your mother," The Queen said. "I think she even wore a dress just like the one you're wearing during her last visit here."

"You are right about the dress Your Highness," Demitri said. "In fact it's the exact dress. We found it some years ago. I couldn't bear to part with it. Seeing her daughter wear the dress is just like going back in time."

"Are you saying this is my mother's dress?" I asked, choking back tears. "It means a lot to me to be wearing something of hers. Thank you."

"My dear, I haven't seen your father. Could he not make the celebration?" The King asked looking around the room.

"I am sorry Your Majesty, my father had other commitments that he had to take care of. But I will tell him you asked about him," I explained, hoping they believed me.

"Well, when you do see your father, please tell him to come by the palace. It has been a while since we have talked," said the King. "Prince Demitri, you have outdone yourself once again with another fine feast. My complements to your chef."

"It's my pleasure, Your Majesty. Even though I would love to have Phoebe living here with her sister and I as she once did, I understand and respect her decision. However, I do miss her. I have always thought of Phoebe and Pheonna as daughters."

"Did we hear our names?" Phoebe and Pheonna asked in unison.

Our table was on a platform facing everyone. Pheonna and Phoebe sat in the center of the table, with Demitri next to them. I sat to his other side with Nessa was beside me and on the other side of the twins sat the Royal family.

While we enjoyed the fabulous feast, I watched Phoebe and Pheonna as they talked and ate. I wondered how two sisters who seemed so close could live so far apart. It broke my heart. I could see how deeply they cared for one another. Maybe this year would be different for them. Maybe my friends and I could find a way to change their situation and keep them together. As I thought of my friends, I wondered where Deena and Sky were, and if they had found Cozmo.

As dinner came to an end, I was feeling a little tired. Nessa excused herself from the table to go sit and talk to her brother and Phoenix who were seated at another table. I saw the three of them get up, and it looked as though they were joining a group to tour the castle. They waved for me to join them, but I shook my head and waved them to go on without me. I noticed that Demitri and I were the only ones left at our table. I had not even realized when everyone else left.

Demitri gently grabbed my hands, looked deep into my eyes and said, "I think I promised you a private tour of my home."

I stood and we walked out into the hallway where all his family portraits hung. He began telling me stories about each one. I listened, wondering if he had walked these same halls with my mother.

"Let me guess," Demitri said as we walked, "You are wondering if I did this with your mother when she was here."

"Let ME guess," I responded, "You must be reading my thoughts just like my friends Glitz and Deena do."

"I do have the ability to read minds, but I did not do that with you. I just know that if I were in your position that's what I would be thinking. And, the answer is YES, I did. You most likely want to know how we met and how well I knew your mother and father. Well, I knew your mother before she even met your father. Our family ties go way back. My family had known her family for centuries. I always thought very highly of Morinda. She was a remarkable woman. Your father on the other hand is a different story. We met during your mother's last adventure, and I'm sorry to say, I doubt am your father's favorite person."

Demitri was about to tell me more about my parent's last adventure, when Pheonna came to us. "Excuse me My Prince, but I need to speak to you in private."

"Anything wrong with our guests?" he asked

"No. Oh but Murranda, I found your friends. They are in the library with my sister. My pet, Neeko, will show you the way." She pointed down to a Siamese cat that looked at me with an evil grin.

"Thank you," I said, "I need to go to them. I will leave you both to talk. Demitri, thank you for the tour. I hope we can continue later."

He nodded and the two of them turned down a corridor while I followed the cat. *I do hope Deena and Sky found Cozmo, and he is okay.* I couldn't wait to tell them some of the things I learned about my family. I wondered how much more there was to the mystery.

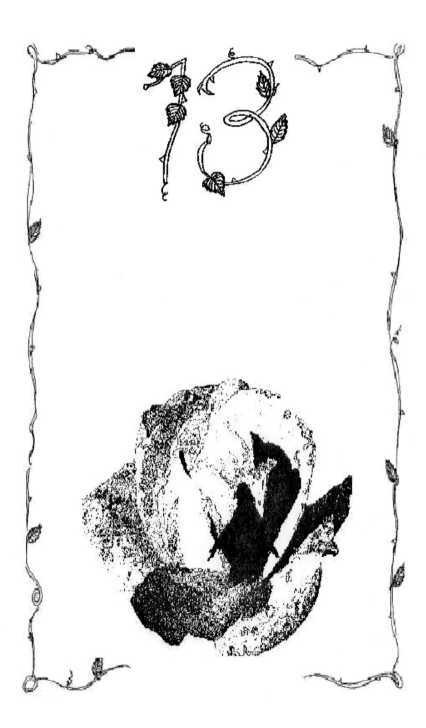

CHAPTER 13

Neeko sauntered his way down the hallway. As we were walking, I noticed that everyone seemed to be watching me, as if they were talking about me. It made me feel a little uncomfortable.

I couldn't worry about that now. I needed to get to my friends. When we and I arrived in front of the library door, I started to kneel down to thank Neeko, but he just hissed and ran off.

As I opened the library door, I heard what sounded like Deena and Phoebe talking about me. I couldn't make out everything they were saying. I walked in to find out what was going on.

I found them standing between two book stacks. "So this is why my ears were burning. You two were talking about me, weren't you?" I said looking around the room.

"We were not talking about you," Deena replied looking at Phoebe. "We were just saying that we needed to let you know we found Cozmo. We knew how badly you wanted to find him. Why anyone would want that oversized feather pillow, I don't know."

"Okay, I'll bite. Where is Cozmo? Why isn't he with you?" I asked looking around suspiciously.

Phoebe came and put her arm around my shoulder and said, "I don't think your friend needs rescuing. Maybe I should say I don't think he wants to be rescued."

"What is that supposed to mean?"

"Come, follow me. I'll show you," said Deena. She led us out of the library into a secret corridor that led to a room with a small sliding peephole. I slid it open and couldn't believe what I was seeing.

It was Cozmo on a pile of silk and velvet pillows, being fed grapes and seeds by some of the prince's servants. I could tell that he was getting on some of the servants' nerves by the way they looked at him and each other.

As I scanned the room, I also noticed Sky was beside him with his tail over the owl's full stomach like a blanket. Deena motioned for us to come out of the corridor and back into the library.

"As you can see, we can leave now and not worry about that overgrown, obnoxious fool. We will just find a way of getting Sky out of there so we can find the others and leave."

"What do you mean leave, Deena?"

"I mean, we can leave this celebration and continue on with your journey. You still want to find whatever it's you are looking for, don't you? There are so many people here no one will miss us. So let's just gather the others and go."

"Deena, there is still so much celebration left here at the castle. You know it's the weekend of peace so what is the rush?" asked Phoebe with a strange look in her eye.

"Phoebe is right, Deena. There is so much going on here that I haven't seen yet," I said as I rubbed her forehead. "Plus, I am learning so much about my family, things my father never told me. The Prince is being especially nice to me. Did you know that the Prince knew my mother for years? His family and hers go back for centuries. I need to know more, and who is to say that what I am looking for is not right here in this castle." I stopped rubbing her head and paced the floor.

"I don't care what your plans are. If you and the others want to leave, that is fine, but I am staying to learn more. Phoebe is here and will make sure I am okay. Anyway, my necklace has not warned me of any danger, so I think you are just overreacting."

"Murry is right, Deena. I will not let anything happen to her. You have my word." Phoebe said still giving Deena a strange look. I couldn't help but wonder what was going on between them.

"But Phoebe, you cannot be with her every minute," Deena said sternly. "You know what could happen here. "

"Deena, please stay with me and enjoy this weekend. I don't really know what I am looking for or where it is, so we are in no rush. Besides, you told me how you promised my mother that you would always look after me and my family, so you cannot leave me."

Deena looked at me with a defeated expression and said, "I will stay."

At that point Sky walked in through the front of the library.

"I thought I was never going to get out of that room. Why did we have to look for that crazy bird? Hey Murry, I almost did not recognize you. You look amazing in that dress."

"You do look beautiful in that dress, Murranda. Just like your mother," said Deena.

"So, what is going on with Cozmo? Why do they have him in there, and why is he living the life of luxury?" I asked.

"Well, they're fattening him up to use him as the trophy for the games tomorrow. I guess they figured if they treated like a king he'd stay in there willingly. And boy is he eating it up." Sky explained.

"I see he still hasn't learned his lesson," Phoebe said rolling her eyes and shaking her head.

"What do you mean?" I asked.

"Let's just say, I am the one who is trying to make him learn," she said.

"Wait, YOU are? He told us a sorceress did that to him."

"I am sure he thinks I am the sorceress since I'm the one who changed him. His greed was out of control and was going to do more harm than good. It seems he still has not learned from his experience."

I had to laugh at this whole thing. Cozmo had us believing Pheonna, the Dark Sorceress, turned him when in fact it was Phoebe.

"You see Deena, we have to stay. Matter of fact let's compete in the game festivities tomorrow and see if we can win Cozmo. That way he will have to come with us when we do leave after the weekend of peace. Besides, I have always wanted to go to a masquerade ball. When I was a little girl, my father would host them at our estate, but I was always too young to attend. Please, it has always been a dream of mine."

Deena looked at me and saw the desperation in my eyes. "How can I say no. I am sure you had your father wrapped around your finger with that face. But, we will leave the morning after the weekend. However, if I see that your necklace senses any form of danger, we will leave immediately. Agreed?"

"Yes, yes, yes! Whatever you say. Thank you! Thank you," I said.

"Well it's getting late, and we have found Cozmo who does not seem to be in any danger now, so why don't we all just turn in for the night."

Phoebe grabbed my wrist and pulled me towards her. "Murry, can we talk for a bit, maybe get some air? I would love to talk to you about your father and Jeffery. If you don't mind."

She turned and looked at Deena

"Sure, go ahead," said Deena. "Sky, let's see if we can find Glitz, Phoenix and the elves. I hear our friend Phoenix has really grown up fast."

When they were gone, Phoebe and I opened the doors in the library and walked out onto the veranda.

"What did you want to tell me about my father and Jeffery?" I asked. "Maybe you want to tell me how you know them and why my father never once mentioned you in any of his stories. I don't mean to sound so upset, but maybe I am a little. Since I have been in this castle, I have heard things about my family that I don't understand. My father and I have always been so close and have shared everything together. I feel I don't know my family as well as I have always believed. That is the real reason I have to stay here. I know there are more secrets about my family here, and I need to know what they are. I must somehow get that across to Deena."

I looked deep into Phoebe's eyes with a tear in mine and said, "If you know anything more about my family, *please* Phoebe, you have to tell me. Don't keep anything from me no matter how much it might hurt or scare me. I am a big girl and I deserve to know the truth. I can see in your eyes that you know more than you have been telling me."

"We just want to protect you Murry," Phoebe said as she wiped my tears away with a silk handkerchief.

I turned away from Phoebe and faced towards the veranda's ledge. "What is everyone protecting me from?" I asked.

I looked down from the veranda and saw Demitri walking on the grounds. "Are you trying to protect me from the Prince? From what he has told me, I get the feeling he cared for my mother and maybe she cared for him. But I am not my mother. I may look like her, but I am not she. I can promise you that I have no intention of pursuing any kind of romance with him. I know he is evil and not to be trusted, but for this weekend he can be. Allow me the chance to learn what I can about my mother."

I headed towards the doors. I wanted to see if I could catch up with Demitri outside.

Phoebe could tell what I was about to do. She grabbed my wrist. "Murry, I really wish you would try and avoid the prince, for your own safety."

"I understand what you are saying Phoebe, but as you can see, the necklace is not warning me of any kind of danger. So, if you will not let me walk out of the room, I will just have to catch up with him this way." I snatched my arm away and jumped onto the veranda's ledge then I flung myself to the nearest tree and began to climb down.

The Prince looked up and saw what was going on and laughed. He floated up to where I was on the tree and helped me down.

"Some people might say that was not very lady like of you, but I found it quite impressive."

All I could do was laugh and turn red. "My father and I have always had issues about me acting ladylike. He liked for me to wear fancy dresses for dinner, but I always preferred to wear pants and blouses,"

"Just like your mother," he said.

Phoebe stood on the veranda watching the prince and I walk away. Jezzica suddenly appeared and stood next to Phoebe on the library veranda.

"You have to ask yourself, if she claims not to want to be involved with the Dark Prince, knowing who he is and what he's capable of—why is she spending so much time with him?" She said with a smirk.

"I trust Murry to be careful around him. This weekend he has sworn to keep the peace, so I know she is safe for now. If you don't mind, Jezzica, I should return to my sister. It's getting late, and there is still a lot to do to get ready for the game and the Masquerade Ball tomorrow."

Phoebe gently pushed Jezzica aside as she passed. Jezzica looked back toward the veranda. "Something tells me that your precious Murry might not be as safe as you think. Our Prince missed his chance once before, and if I know him, he will not fail again."

She slowly vanished into thin smoke.

CHAPTER 14

𝒫rince Demitri and I walked through the grounds. I couldn't believe how beautiful, yet utterly frightening it was out here. Even the moon gave me an eerie feeling as it peeked over the nearby lake. It gave the water a purplish glow.

The blowing wind sounded like a mixture of wolves' howls and an eerie hum. It gave me chills. *How could a place so beautiful hold so much evil and danger?*

Demitri noticed my shiver and thought I was cold. He removed his cape and wrapped it around me.

"Thank you," I said as we continued walking. "Tell me more about my mother. You mentioned that your families went back centuries. Can you tell me more about that?" I leaned against a tree that seemed to be standing in front of the full purplish moon.

"How much do you know about your mother?" asked Demitri. "You said she died in childbirth. What has your father told you about her?"

He leaned against the tree and stood very close to me. I looked down toward the ground.

Finally I replied, "Because of Father's stories, I thought I knew everything there was to know about my mother. He told me how they met and about their many adventures, plans and dreams. However, in the short time I've been here, I feel that I don't really know them at all. I never knew they had met you or that they knew Phoebe. I can't understand why he would have kept that from me."

I looked at Demitri with a tear in my eye. He wiped away the tear with his cold finger and said, "Maybe he had his reasons. Are you certain you want to know more about the connection your mother and I had and what took place the last time she was here?"

Suddenly, my necklace began to vibrate and the ruby on the necklace glowed brighter and brighter. I put my hand over the stone to hide the glow from him.

"Demitri, I think we need to leave. I feel as though someone or something does not want us here." I grabbed his hand and started back toward the castle. I was so confused.

Demitri followed me away, but stopped me in front of the castle entrance.

"Wait Murranda! Calm down! There is nothing to be afraid of. Listen to me. I know your necklace is warning you about something, but you're overreacting. You really don't want your friends to see you like this."

I paused. "Like what?" I asked.

"Startled," replied Demitri. "Also, they shouldn't see your necklace glowing like that. I know what the necklace can do. I know the power it has. If your friends see it this way they will surely want to make you leave, and I know you don't want to do that."

He was right. If my friends thought there was any danger, they would try to force me to leave this place.

"How can we hide this bright glow from them?" I asked as I tried to hide the glowing stone with my hands. "I do want to stay and learn more about my mother. I believe I can do that here. For some reason, my friends don't want me to learn more about her. I wish I knew why."

"I have an idea," Demitri said. He grabbed my hands and held them to his cold chest. "But, you will have to trust me."

I knew my friends would advise me against it. But, he is the only one that is opening up to me about my mother. He is telling me things my father and Jeffery kept from me. If I want to know more, I had no choice. I *had* to trust him.

He leaned in closer and opened his hand, as if by magic, an identical stone appeared. "You must give me the stone from the necklace and replace it with this one. It's a perfect match."

Could we really pull this off? Would anyone notice the switch?

"Murranda, you've lived your whole life in a box. Everyone around you has been afraid to let you go out on your own. There has always been someone around to protect you. This is your chance to finally fly. No ropes to hold you down or net to catch you when you fall. You can show everyone that you can pick yourself up and do this."

He leaned in closer to my ear. "Look around you, Murranda. You're really not on your own yet. You have seven bodyguards called friends, and even without them, you have this necklace and ring to warn you and protect you from danger. They are just another kind safety net, they are a rope tying you down. BREAK FREE Murranda."

Demitri was right. My friends mean well, just as my father does, but I have to make this journey on my own and on my own terms, not only to prove to them but to myself as well. I nodded my head in agreement.

He put his hand over the ruby once and the stone vanished. Then he put his hand over the setting again and a look-alike was in its place. There was a part of me that still felt uneasy about this, and Demitri could see that.

"You are probably wondering if I am doing this so I can steal the stone because of its power. Here, you can keep it in this." He handed me the glowing stone and a silk pouch. Once I put the stone into the pouch, you couldn't see the glow anymore. I put the pouch in my small purse.

It was very late now, so Demitri walked me into the castle and back to my room.

When we arrived at my door, I was still feeling uneasy. Could we really fool anyone with this look-a-like stone? Why was the stone glowing in the first place? What was it trying to warn me of? Was Demitri the reason my necklace began to glow?

He was right about one thing: I was tired of everyone trying to protect me from everything. I am old enough and capable enough to take care of myself. This was my journey to begin with. I like having the company of my new friends, but this is my destiny.

"I sense you are still worried about why the necklace was glowing and concerned that your friends will find out. You really need to trust me, and act as if everything is okay. Have you had any training in the art of acting?" he asked.

I nodded my head yes.

"Well then, you need to give your best performance and act as though everything is fine. I know you can do it if you truly want to stay and learn more about yourself and your family. I will tell you everything you want and need to know, but you have to make your friends believe that everything is okay. Plus, I would love to see just how well you do with a sword during the competition. Perhaps I could share a dance or two with you that night during the Masquerade Ball." He lifted my head and looked deep into my eyes.

"Until then Murranda, sweet dreams. Your friends are waiting for you in the next room, It's best that you not keep them waiting any longer."

He leaned in closer. I could feel his cold breath on my lips, as if he were going to kiss them, but instead he kissed my cheek and vanished into thin air. I turned away and quickly open the door to my room.

Just as he had said, there were all my friends sitting on or around my bed waiting for me; Sky, Glitz, Flutter, Deena, Jett, Nessa, Phoenix, and Phoebe.

"What's going on here?" I asked, closing the door behind me

"We were just talking," said Glitz as he came up and hugged me.

"About what? Or do I have to ask?" I said, looking straight at Deena. "Let me see if I can guess. Deena has been talking, and you are all in agreement that I should leave this castle and the Shadow Land in the middle of this weekend's celebration; the same celebration that is given in honor of you, Phoebe, and your sister. As you can see, my necklace is not warning me of danger. Why? Because there is no danger to warn about."

I hoped they would believe me and not notice that the stone on my necklace had been replaced.

"We all understand what this weekend represents Murry," said Deena walking up to me. "But, what do you think you are going to find here?"

"Deena is right," added Phoebe. "What is here that you need to find?"

"When I first met you at the gypsy fair Phoebe, wasn't it you who told me that even though I knew about the Shadow Land and all its dangers, I would still have to come here? You all know that the reason I'm on this journey is to look for something I know in my heart I need to find. If you all want to leave, you can. But I am staying for the whole weekend."

I paced nervously.

"Besides, as I told Deena earlier, since I was a little girl I have always wanted to attend a Masquerade Ball. If I haven't found what I am looking for by the time the celebration has ended and everyone else has gone, I will then, and only then continue my journey. I do desperately want to find whatever it is. But for now, THIS conversation is over. I would like to get ready for bed. Tomorrow is a big day, and we all should get some sleep."

As I paced around the room, I began to notice things: how Glitz and Flutter were acting together and how Jett couldn't keep his eyes off of Phoenix. It seemed as though love was in the air. It made it hard for me to be angry. I thought it was so cute, and I was happy for all four of them. I had to smile when they each came to give me a goodnight hug or kiss.

When everyone had gone, I closed my door and felt a touch of envy towards them. I thought how nice it would be to find someone to love. Perhaps I will find love somewhere during this journey. Maybe that is what I was being drawn to.

CHAPTER 15

I looked around my room. It made me homesick. I thought about how I missed feeding the ducks and swans while walking along the lake and how much I enjoyed horseback riding, not only during the day but also late at night with only the light from the moon and stars.

I remembered how during Christmas, I would take the horses out in the snow. My father, Jeffery and I would hitch up the family sled to the horses and string bells around the sled and on the horses and go for a ride into town. There we would bundle up the orphans and take them for a ride, and then we all would drink hot chocolate and sing carols.

I thought about my father and Jeffery back at Phoebe's place in the gypsy fair. I wondered if they were still there or if they woke to find Phoebe gone. They would probably be very angry. I pray they are still okay, and that they understand why I needed them to stay put. Phoebe was only doing what she knew I wanted.

While everyone slept, Pheonna was in her lair pouring green liquid into a marble bowl.

"Water of green, reveal to me what I wish to see," she chanted. A reflection of Murranda appeared in her room.

"As I turn back time during this past day, my water of green reveal to me all that she has seen."

As if by magic, the water showed her all that Murry had done since she entered the castle. When Pheonna saw the time Murry and the prince spent together it did not sit well with her. She could see how close the prince felt toward the girl. She could also tell that even if Murry did not realize it, she had feelings for the prince.

"This cannot be!" she exclaimed. "I was hoping that once I got him away from Morinda years ago, he would turn his affection towards me. Then I would rule beside him. Now this Murry girl is spoiling my plans. This time I will not be as nice. Instead of just ridding her from the castle like I did her mother, I will get rid of her altogether." She said, pressing her palms together.

"First, I must see how she really feels about him and I must find her weakness. Whatever I do to get rid of her must be done in such a way that it will never be traced back to me, even if it means this will be the last celebration for my sister and I. As much as I love my sister Phoebe, what I love more is the fact that once I get rid of Murranda, I can turn the prince's heart toward me. Then we can rule the Shadow Land together." Pheonna let out an evil laugh.

She called for her two minions, "Jezzica, Emily!" Immediately two spiders appeared beside her. The spiders spun their web upward transforming themselves into female bodies.

"Yes, my lady," the sisters said simultaneously.

"I need you two to get close to this girl while she is staying with us. Become her new friends, her confidants."

"I have already spent time with her, my lady," said Jezzica. "She knows me, and I think she trusts me. I also did my usual due diligence on all our guests, so I know some things about her. One thing she loves to do is go late-night horseback riding"

"That is perfect. Listening to Murranda talk to her friends, I get the feeling that she is restless.

Maybe a nice ride around the grounds will help. Get to know her better. Find out how she likes it here and what her feelings are toward our prince. Also, find out what she and her friends are planning to do once they leave here. Find out all you can and report back to me before sunrise."

"Yes, my lady," Jezzica and Emily said.

They walked out of Pheonna's room and Emily whispered to Jezzica, "Maybe we can also find out more about Murry's elf friend, Jett."

"I was thinking the same thing, my sister," replied Jezzica.

CHAPTER 16

Meanwhile at the gypsy camp, Rudy and Jeffrey, awakened from what they thought was a short nap. Jeffrey stood and looked outside. He noticed that the sun was beginning to rise.

"I guess we were more tired than we thought my Lord. We slept through the whole night."

"We did?" Rudy said gazing out the window to see if it was true. "Then we truly need to be on our way if we are going to find my daughter."

Sheila came out from behind the curtain separating the rooms. "Well, I see you two finally woke up. I guess the elixir she put in your food did not quite last the entire two weeks."

"WHAT DID YOU SAY?" asked Rudy loudly. "Are you telling me that we have been asleep for almost two weeks, and our old friend did this to us?"

"Oops! I was not supposed to say that."

Sheila quickly hid behind the curtain. "But, she did tell me to give you these letters when you woke up." She pointed her boney finger toward the table.

"Where did she go, or do I really have to ask?" Sheila hid behind the curtain fold.

"She went to the Shadow Land for the celebration reunion with her sister. That's where Murry is! She's keeping me away from my own daughter when she needs me most. How dare she do this to me! She knows I have already lost my beloved wife, and now she is keeping me from protecting my Sunshine. Jeffery, get the horse and cart. We're leaving now!

"I am one step ahead of you, sir. Whenever you are ready we can leave. Sir, how can we get there in time. It's more than a few days' journey." Jeffery said, gathering their belongings and putting them into the cart.

"I don't care how long it takes. We are going to find my little girl and bring her home. She may get mad at me for putting an end to this journey, but she will thank me later." Rudy grabbed his coat and hopped on the cart, taking the reins.

Sheila came running from the tent with something in her hands. "WAIT! This may help you get to her faster." She opened her hands and held out a tiny bird. "This bird will lead you to Phoebe and your daughter."

"Why should we trust any of you? You all kept us here for almost two weeks knowing where my only child was. You had to know the dangers she would face when she entered the Shadow Land, and more important, the Dark Castle with the Dark Prince." Rudy said. He angrily pushed the bird away.

The bird suddenly called out, "Phoebe, Phoebe."

"Maybe this gypsy lady is right, Sir. The bird keeps calling Phoebe's name. Maybe it wants us to find her. What would it hurt? It's not like we know where to go. Let's follow her sir."

Jeffery leaned over and grabbed the tiny bird before it could fly away.

"Set the bird free and it will find Phoebe," explained Sheila. "I don't know how, but the two of them have a connection. Trust me. If anyone can find Phoebe, this little bird can. Once you find your way to Phoebe, you will also find your daughter."

Rudy looked at Sheila and said, "We will follow the bird, but if anything has happened to my little sunshine, I am holding Phoebe and all of you responsible."

Jeffery set the bird free again. It flew around in circles, gathering its bearings and flying toward a path to the south.

"You see, Sir, it looks like we have a winged blood hound instead of a four-legged blood hound. It's going in the direction of Elvinnia. I remember that place." Rudy and Jeffery began following the bird, hoping it would lead them to their dear Murranda.

"I cannot believe that we must trust a bird to lead us to my Sunshine. If anything has happened to my only child, SOMEONE WILL PAY. I have already lost the love of my life. Damned if I am going to lose my only child." Rudy looked down at the rose to get a view of what his daughter was doing, but more importantly, to see if there was anything that could tell him where she was.

He noticed that she appeared to be in a very fancy room. He studied the rose more intently and knew exactly where Murry was! She was in a castle, but not just any castle. He knew in his gut that his daughter was at the Dark Castle in the Shadow Land. Rudy was convinced Murranda was with the Dark Prince and the Sorceress. He was certain that his daughter's life was in danger.

"Look, Jeffrey, why are we following this silly bird. We can see in the rose that Murry is at the Dark Castle, and we both know where that is. Let's just forget about the bird and just head there."

"My Lord, I truly think it's best that we follow the bird and go where he is taking us. If she's at the Dark Castle, the bird will lead us there. If it really has been two weeks, then this is the weekend of peace at and the celebration of the Two Sisters is still going on."

"You'd better be right, old friend. The prince and the sorceress knew the truth about my beloved, so they must also know about my sunshine. I just pray they haven't revealed it to her. She will never forgive me. I was only trying to protect her from all of this. I don't care what was written in the past. I don't want her to ever discover the truth. I just hope I am not too late. If she does find out, I hope I can still save her," Rudy cried.

"So do I, my Lord, so do I!"

17

CHAPTER 17

*J*ezzica and her sister Emily were carrying out Pheonna's request to get close to and gain Murranda's trust. They came up with a plan to get Murranda out of the room in secret.

"Go and gather the horses sister, while I see if Murranda is in her room and what she is doing," Jezzica whispered to Emily.

"Why do I have to go get the horses like some servant? Why can't you?"

"Fine! You climb up the tree and tear your pretty dress and maybe run into some of her friends. Let them see you all a mess. I was just trying to be nice and save you the embarrassment, sister."

"Oh yes, and I suppose Jett might be up there talking to her now. Okay, I will get the horses, but let me know if you see the elf boy."

"I wonder what she knows about the elf boy? If my little sister thinks she can take him from me, she has another think coming. I ALWAYS get what I want! ALWAYS! I cannot believe I fooled her again with that climbing up a tree and getting your dress torn bit." Jezzica laughed.

"Will she ever learn that we SpiderVamps don't need to climb. We just reach the top of anything like this!" Jezzica pointed her fingers up towards the tree next to where Murry's room was.

A shiny, glittery web shot from her fingertips onto the highest branch of the tree. She grabbed the other end, and pulled herself up. Jezzica knew she couldn't let Murry or her friends see her spying on them. She transformed herself back into a spider.

She jumped off the tree and sat on the porch ledge where she watched what was going on between Murry and her friends. She eavesdropped, listening as they tried to convince Murry to leave the castle even before the weekend of peace was over.

Jezzica noticed Jett seemed to be getting close to the girl next to him. Jezzica was not pleased. She was so upset that the "X" on her back began getting redder and redder. All of Murry's friends began to leave, and Murry finally was alone in her room. That is when she knew it was time to do what the sorceress wanted.

Jezzica transformed back into her vamp form and crept toward the room.

I prepared for bed, thinking about my mother. I wished she were alive and here with me now. I also thought about my father, wondering why he had kept so many secrets from me. What was it he was trying to protect me from? I was puzzled as to why I felt so at home in the dark castle when everyone I knew was afraid of it. I felt I had been here before and that this was where I belonged. Why was Demitri acting so sweet and gentlemanly towards me?

I heard a knock at my window. I walked over and found Jezzica floating just outside the edge of the balcony.

"How long have you been out there?" I asked, opening the balcony door.

"I've been here for a while. I could see that you and your friends were having a discussion, so I did not want to disturb you. I came hoping you could accompany me and my sister on a late night horseback ride."

"Sure, I would love to. Where are the horses and your sister?" Jezzica pointed down to where two horses were ready and waiting. "I'd better get changed out of these and back into my regular clothes."

"What you're wearing is fine," said Jezzica.

"Well then, let's go downstairs."

"Why take the stairs? We can go down the same way I came up."

Jezzica pointed her two fingers at me. A web shot from her fingers and around my waist. With the other hand she sent a web onto the tree like a rope to take us down.

"Wait! How did you do that? I thought you were a vampire?" I asked in confusion.

"We are known as Spider Vamps," a voice replied. I looked on the back of one of the horses and saw a spider that appeared to be laughing at me.

The spider then quickly turned itself into a young girl with long, brown hair. She looked just like Jezzica.

"Well, well, well! You must be Murranda. The whole castle is talking about you, especially the prince. I am Emily, and I see you already know my sister Jezzica." Emily handed me a set of reigns.

"Here, you can ride the prince's prize horse, Mystic. Be careful! She can be a little feisty. My sister and I will ride Thunder. We would love to show you around the Shadow Land."

"Are you sure it's safe?" I asked looking around and hearing all the howling and other night noises.

"Don't worry, Murry," said Jezzica "With us at your side nothing will happen. Also, everyone here knows that the penalty for trying to hurt or kill someone this weekend is a very painful death. Plus, I've noticed the prince and others in the castle are very fond of you."

"So, what are we waiting for?" asked Emily. "Let's go riding."

I mounted the horse and the three of us went for a moonlight ride. It was quite breathtaking yet at the same time, very haunting. The wind blew through the trees making a humming, howling noise as the leaves shook.

Jezzica and Emily directed my attention to the different points of interest in Shadow Land. They showed me where the many creatures lived; some in caves, some in huts, some in cottages and others in the open swamp.

There were skeleton bones lying around, crows flying and buzzards trying to find an old carcass for food. It was all pretty creepy and yet, intriguing.

"Murry, as we told you, it seems to us and others in the castle that the dark prince has found favor with you. I was wondering, how do you feel about him?" Jezzica asked. "Are the two of you getting close? Not that I would mind."

"I am sure I know some of the ones who don't like the fact that the prince and I have been spending time together," I said sarcastically. "I really don't know how I feel about him. Everyone has been telling me that Demitri is evil and dangerous, but he has been nothing but a gentleman with me. All I know is that he has told me things about my mother that my father had not shared with me. I want to learn everything the prince knows about my family, and no one is going to stop me."

"I don't understand why my father never told me about the Shadow Land and the Dark Castle or the Prince. When Glitz was at my house helping to build the Labyrinth Garden, we were talking about all the places we might go to on this journey. Glitz mentioned that we would need to avoid the Shadow

Land and the Dark Castle. My father acted as if he had never heard of this place. But the stories I am hearing from the prince and the fact that the people and creatures that live here mistook me for my mother let me know that my father was very much aware of all of it. None of this makes sense." I said in frustration.

"This whole thing is so confusing to me. If what the Prince is saying about my family is true, why would my father make me believe that he had never heard of this place. But if my father really never heard of the Dark Castle or the Prince what would Demitri have to gain by lying to me. I have to stay to find the truth. Perhaps these secrets are what my whole journey has been about; to find out the truth about my family. I am going to know everything I can about Demitri and this place and all he seems to know about my mother. And NO ONE is going to stop me."

"You don't have to preach to us," said Emily. "My sister and I think you are doing the right thing. If you and the prince do become closer, we will not view that as a bad thing. We could all have a lot of fun together even after the weekend of peace. There is so much we can show and teach you about the Shadow Land and the power it holds. Some of us *are* hoping that you and Demitri get closer. We all feel about you the same way we felt about your mother. She was an amazing woman, and we can see that her spirit rests within you. But I always say, when it comes to love it does not matter what other people want or worry about. The heart wants what the heart wants and nothing should stand in the way of love."

"Well, I have to admit, I do find Demitri intriguing." I said as I turned my head and blushed. "When I am around him I feel like I can just talk to him for hours. I also feel that I have known him all my life."

As Emily, Jezzica and I rode the horses around the shadow land I thought about my mother. It seems as though the longer I'm here, the closer my connection to her is becoming.

I began to feel eyes watching me. Not just the evil ones within Shadow Land, but also my so called friends. I know they mean well and love me and are worried about me. But, I wish they could just trust my judgment about what is best for me.

I wish my friends would turn their focus off of the prince and me and back on what we are going to do about the owl Cozmo. How were we going to win the games tomorrow?

While the three of us were riding and having a great time I noticed someone standing in the distance. So far no one had noticed that the necklace had been changed. I know the necklace was warning me about something, But I feel safe here. I know deep down I need to stay and find out all that I can about my family.

As we rode closer, Demitri was standing there by the very same tree where we had been earlier that evening.

I looked over at Jezzica and asked, "Did you plan this little encounter for me and the prince?" I looked back at where he was standing but he was gone. Suddenly, he appeared sitting behind me causing me to jump.

"No they did not plan this," Demitri said, reaching around to grab the horse's reins and pull us to a stop "but I noticed that someone had taken my horse and one of the others. So I did a little mind control and guided the horses this way. I hope you don't mind? Emily, Jezzica if you two could please take the horses back to the stables I would like to spend some time with Murranda." He helped me off the horse and handed the reins to Jezzica.

"As you wish my Prince," they said in unison. The two girls and the horses vanished into thin air.

Demitri took my hand and we walked along the lake back to the castle. "I do hope you are enjoying your stay here. Did you enjoy your ride with Jezzica and Emily? I hope you were not frightened by the night creatures. They are supposed to be on their best behavior this weekend."

"The ride was very nice, eerie, but nice. I like Jezzica and Emily. I've never met anyone like them. I've never even heard of SpiderVamps."

"They are a rare breed indeed," Demitri explained. "No one really knows how they came about. They are very secretive about their heritage, but they have shown themselves to be very useful in my kingdom. Everyone in my kingdom is either family or enemy. If you are an enemy, then you don't live long here. Murranda, can I ask you something? What do you know about your mother besides the adventures she and your father shared? Is there anything else you know about her such as where she came from or her abilities?"

I shrugged my shoulders and looked toward the lake. "I'm afraid I don't know much. Besides the adventures, the only thing I know was that she loved music, writing and gardening. She died when I was born, and I know that it's hard for my father to talk about her. He does try for my sake, so I can have some idea about who my mother was. But the longer I stay here the more I feel that my father has been keeping things about my mother from me, and I don't understand why he would do something like that."

"Maybe he is doing so to protect you in some way," he said as he touched his cold hand to my face and pulled me toward him. "Don't be mad at your father Murranda. There is always a reason for everything, and that reason will come to light soon."

"It's not only my father, Demitri I feel that everyone here is keeping some big secret from me. I don't know why, but I am not leaving until I know what is going on. Maybe this is what I have been looking for. If it's not, then whatever it is I need to find will have to wait until I have learned the truth about my mother and whatever it is about me that seems to have everyone acting strange."

"I understand you want some answers Murranda, but it is quite late and this weekend is a celebration. I would hate for you to miss out on all the fun. Tomorrow the games begin. With all the running, jumping, archery, and sword fighting it should be a lot of fun for you and your friends to watch."

"You think my friends and I are just going to watch? Who said we might not sign up for some of those games? I can shoot a bow and arrow and swing a sword or two." I said with a grin and a giggle.

"Oh, can you now? Then I may just have to sign up as well. And don't worry about your feathered friend. He will be okay. At the end of it all I will make sure that you get him back unharmed."

"Thank you," I said. "I do hope he is not giving your servants a hard time. You see he is not easy to be around. If he comes back with a broken beak, I wouldn't be surprised." I laughed.

Demitri and I kept talking and laughing all the way to my room.

"Thank you for the walk and talk. I hope to do this again soon. I would love for you to tell me ALL that you know about my mother. But unlike you, I do need to get some sleep."

"Until tomorrow sweet Murranda," he said kissing my hand. Then ever so softly he kissed my cheek. I got chills up my back and neck. I turned to open the door and then turned back to say goodnight, but Demitri was gone. Grayish purple smoke lingered where he stood.

I went into my room. My friends including Phoebe, were there waiting for me.

"Where have you been all evening?" asked Phoebe as she sat on one corner of my bed with her arms crossed and giving me that disappointed yet worried look.

"Or the better question should be who were you with?" asked Deena as she walked toward me from my window.

I looked around and saw Jett, Phoenix and Nessa sitting on my bed. A tiger sized Sky was lying on the floor by the foot of my bed, and Glitz and Flutter were on my dresser in their fairy size.

I stretched out my arms and gave a big yawn, "Well, well, look how late it's getting. We all have that festival of games coming in the morning, so we better get some sleep. We can talk about this later."

I gave Deena a hug and opened the door for everyone to leave. "Please trust me when I tell you guys you have nothing to worry about. I went on a moonlight ride with Jezzica and her sister Emily and we happened to run into Prince Demitri. Then he escorted me back to the castle and to my room while the girls took care of the horses."

"WAIT!" Glitz yelled growing to boy size. "You went on a ride with the SpiderVamp Sisters? They are not to be trusted Murry. Don't you know that?"

"Glitz, they were fine. We had a nice time riding and talking. Remember this is the weekend of peace. So NO harm will come to me." Then I kissed him on the forehead.

"Please, we have been through all this already. I am not leaving under any circumstances. I have to learn what they know about my mother. This place and these people hold a lot of secrets, and I am not leaving until I find them all. Maybe this is what I have been searching for anyway. So everyone go to your rooms and get some sleep. We are going to enjoy this reunion celebration for Phoebe and her sister."

"Yes, Murry is right," Sky said walking towards me. He rubbed his head affectionately against my legs.

"There is nothing to worry about this weekend, so let's just enjoy. After this weekend celebration is over, if Murry has not found whatever it is she is looking for here, then we can all leave and continue our journey. Right Murry, once the celebration is over if you still haven't found what it's you are searching for, we can all leave. But until then, we will just enjoy this break."

I looked at Sky, knelt down and gave him a big hug. "That seems fair. We stay for the celebration with no questions asked, and let me just enjoy myself here. If I still haven't found what I am searching for, then we can continue our journey onward. Thanks Sky. You seem to be the only one here on my side. And just for that, if you want, you can sleep here with me on my bed. But first you will need to shrink a little more to about kitten size.

"Sure, I would like that," he said. Then he shrunk from tiger size to kitten size. Everyone else nodded their heads in reluctant agreement, said their goodnights and walked out the door to their own rooms for the rest of the night.

I went into the bathroom to change for bed humming a tune I heard at dinner earlier this evening. "So Murry, just how do you feel about the prince? Not that I am getting on your case or anything, but the sound of your humming makes me think that you are smitten with him," said Sky as he jumped on my bed and looked for a spot to sleep.

"Well Sky, I don't really know how I feel about him, but I do think he is very intriguing and mysterious, but not in a scary way. I think there is more to Demitri then he allows people to see," I said coming out of my bathroom, brushing out my hair.

"For some reason I feel that my mother saw the same things in him that I do. I don't know what it's yet but there is definitely something there. But Sky, it's getting late, so let's just go to bed. We have a lot to do tomorrow." I kissed Sky goodnight and got in my bed.

I put the brush down by my nightstand and went to turn off the light. I didn't see anything there to turn them off. Once I got under my covers, the lights slowly dimmed till they were completely off and the only light in the room came from the full moon outside.

"Good night Sky."

"Good night Murry."

I looked at the picture of my mother and father on the nightstand. "I do hope my father is okay."

"I'm sure he is Murry."

I sighed. "Goodnight Sky."

I kissed the picture.

CHAPTER 18

I fell into a deep sleep moving right into a strange dream. My father and mother were standing in my room. They looked a lot younger. My father was slimmer and did not have his goatee. He was wearing a white ruffled button-down collar and ruffled sleeves. My mother wore a gorgeous blood-red dress with what appeared to be a black and gold spider web overlay. The ends of her black hair had blood-red streaks on them. She was also wearing the same necklace Phoebe gave me.

I looked down to the foot of my bed hoping to see Sky so he could tell me if he was seeing the same thing, but he was nowhere to be found. I called out to my mother because I was so excited to finally meet her. But neither she nor my father could hear me. I could tell they were arguing about something important.

My father was almost yelling. "Why do you need to have dinner alone with the Prince? You know what he is, and you know what he wants. If he does get what he wants, it will be the end of Xeenophillia as we know and love it. The Dark Prince and the Shadow Land would win, and both of our worlds would be in jeopardy." He grabbed both of her shoulders.

"I will be fine Rudy my love. You must trust me. I know what I am doing." Mother took his hands and pressed them against her heart.

"I will not let you go see him!" he yelled and ran to the door to block her from leaving the room.

"You know you cannot stop me my love," she said. It was clear Father knew he couldn't stop her even if he tried. She kissed him on the forehead and suddenly he went into a trance like sleep.

Mother took her right hand and in a wide circular motion formed a cloud that looked like a bed. It scooped Father up and floated him to the bed I was on.

I couldn't believe what I was seeing. My mother had powers just like the people who lived here in this castle. When the floating bed reached me, it went right through me as if one of us were a ghost.

None of this made any sense to me.

Suddenly there was a knock on the door. My mother opened it and found Prince Demitri on the other side.

"You look breathtaking my dear," Demitri said to her as he kissed the back of her gloved hand. "Shall we go to dinner before the ball begins? I arranged a private dinner on my balcony overlooking the lake. With the full moon, I know you will enjoy the view."

Mother bashfully nodded her head yes and they headed out the door. Just before it closed, Demitri looked at me. He gave me a slick smile and a wink that sent chills down my back.

I woke from my dream gasping for breath.

Sky jumped up from her place at the end of the bed. "Are you okay, Murry?" he asked.

"Yes Sky, I am okay. It was just a dream. Go back to sleep."

I laid my head back on my pillow and gave Sky a loving scratch around the neck to assure him I was fine. He settled back into his spot on the bed and went back to sleep. I turned onto my side and thought about the dream. *It had to have been just a dream. My mother couldn't have done all of that to my father. She did not have any unique powers that I know of. Yes, it had to have been just a dream. Sometimes we dream about things we really cannot do but maybe wish we could. It was just my imagination going wild. But it felt SO REAL*, I thought.

And Demitri looked right at me as if he were in control of my dreams. My parents couldn't see me but he could. I know he did. It felt more like a vision than a normal dream. And what did my father mean about both of their worlds?

I drifted back to sleep.

This time my dream took me to a different room in the castle filled with bottles, poisons and other magical items. Instead of seeing my parents or the Prince, I saw Phoebe and Pheonna.

They were talking to each other and seemed to be worried about something, Phoebe more so than Pheonna.

"What are you going to do?" Phoebe asked her sister. "Murranda and the prince seem to be getting too close, and we cannot allow it. Remember what the prince vowed to do with their first born."

"I remember and I do understand that sister dear. For once I agree somewhat." Pheonna said. "I cannot help but think if they do get closer what then? She might break his family's curse. I think it's time for that to happen," she continued "It's time that the Shadow Land gain more power than your precious Xenophillia. The Shadow Land used to be your home, too. But I guess you have forgotten about us."

"No, I haven't forgotten Sister," said Phoebe. "As much as I try to, I cannot forget because of my love for you Pheonna. But I will stop you if you or anyone from this land tries to hurt any of my people."

"These used to be your people. You belong here with me," said Pheonna.

"Not anymore, Sister, and you know why. I will always love you, but my love for the ones I have vowed to watch over and protect means more to me just as the Shadow Land means more to you. I will protect my realm and its people and creatures with my life."

"No worries, Sister," Pheonna assured her. "As I said, I do agree they should not be allowed to get close. If anyone is going to be at the right side of my Dark Prince it shall be ME."

Then Pheonna picked up what looked like a Murry Rose. "I will stop at NOTHING to make that happen."

She turned, holding the rose and looked straight at me. My white Murry Rose suddenly turned as black as coal.

CHAPTER 19

I awoke to the sound of someone knocking on my door. When the door opened, it was one of the prince's servants wheeling into my room a long cart with tons of different types of food.

"Room service my lady. I hope you slept well." He was a middle-aged man with dark hair except for a little strip of gray on his right side part. He had pale skin so I knew he was another vampire.

"I slept okay," I said as I sat up on my bed attempting to fix my hair with my fingers as best as I could.

"Are you sure, my lady? You look as if you have been tossing and turning." I was given a plate of food.

"This should help you. The prince is having all his guests served breakfast in bed while the other servants help get things ready for the games. I know this looks like a lot of food for a woman of your petite size, but not to worry, some of your friends wish to have breakfast with you so they asked me to bring their food here. If, that is okay with you my lady." I nodded.

"They should be on their way soon. I passed your feline friend in the hall on my way in here. I assume he was going to get the others."

I looked at where Sky had been sleeping and saw that he was no longer there.

"Yes that would be lovely."

"You and your friends enjoy your breakfast. Feel free to take your time. We will let everyone know when the arena is ready. Oh, before I forget my lady, the prince asked me to give you this. He thought you might like it." He pulled a beautiful purple rose that sparkled from inside his jacket. "He said it was as unique as you are."

"Thank you." I blushed and smiled "I mean, please tell his highness thank you and that I love it."

"Yes my lady, I will do so. But may I say I can see why the prince has shown so much favor toward you and how he is so taken by your beauty. This rose pales in comparison to your beauty my lady even in the morning when you have just awakened."

I turned my head and blushed even more. "I can see that this Casanova charm does not only come from the prince. I guess all vampires have this ability in them. Perhaps the stories I've heard or read about vampires and the way mortals cannot resist them are true. Well, thank you for all your help here. Now if you don't mind, I would like to freshen up before my friends come in and join me for this lovely breakfast."

The servant bowed his head and left the room. I got out of bed and poured myself some juice. I took it with me to the bathroom where I showered and got myself ready for my friends. I decided to go ahead and put on the cloths I was going to wear to compete in the games. I needed something flexible, yet fashionable. I couldn't wait to compete.

Once I got out of the bathroom and put my cloths on, I started drying my hair with a towel in one hand and drinking my juice with the other.

I walked and sat back on my bed next to the food. "Did anyone say breakfast?" Nessa asked walking into the room. I hugged her.

"Good Morning Murry. I don't know about you but I am starving," she said starting on the fruit bowl. After her came Deena and Sky. Glitz and Flutter flew past them all, and once inside, raised their arms and grew to their little child-like size.

"Wow! Look at all this food," Glitz exclaimed. "They are really trying to fatten us up right before the tournament starts.

Glitz was right. There was a lot of food. There was a huge basket of apples, carrots and oats that seemed to be for Deena. I picked up the basket and set it in front of her. On a large wooden board, there were all different kinds of meats, some raw and some semi-roasted. That seemed to be for Sky. Nessa helped me pick up the wooden board of food and set it in front of Sky. Then there was a bushel of honey suckles and some veggie and boysenberries for Glitz and Flutter. There was cooked fowl, veggies and exotic fruits for Nessa, and finally there were some pastries and eggs Benedict for me.

While we were enjoying this huge feast, we started talking about the different types of games they might have at the arena today. Then Deena looked up at me with concern in her eyes "SO have you had any more run ins with the prince?"

"Can we not start that again," I said looking at her with frustration.

"I only asked because I am concerned about you," she exclaimed. "I told you how I knew your mother and how all the unicorns like myself vowed to her that we would *always* look after her and her family and since you are her only child I have to ask."

"I know you and the others are very concerned about me and the prince, but be assured there is *nothing* there. I just want to enjoy this weekend. I know in my heart that the people here, including the prince, know more about my family. And I promise that when I find out everything I can about my mother and my family I will go back home to my father and I will confront him about all these secrets he has been keeping from me."

"Murry!" Deena said looking up at me while she was eating. "Don't get so upset with your father. I am sure what he did or did not do or what he said or did not say about your mother was only because he was trying to protect you just like we are trying to do now. We only have your best interest at heart, and you know what I say is true."

"That may be so Deena." I exclaimed right after I took a big bite of my pastry then tried to chew and talk at the same time. I quickly chewed and swallowed what I was eating took a sip a juice and continued. "But, I am NOT a little child anymore. I don't need to be treated like a delicate porcelain doll. I am not that fragile. I don't need 24-hour protection, plus, how can secrets protect a person. It's time I knew the complete truth about my mother and who I really am. I am not leaving this place until I do."

I got up from my bed and started heading to the door. I reached out to grab the doorknob then turned my head back to my friends and said, "I think I am DONE with this conversation." Before anyone could butt in, I continued, "If you don't mind I am going to get a little air ALONE. Maybe look for Jett and Phoenix and see what they are up to."

As I slammed the door shut, I heard Sky say, "I can see that went well. If we are staying, we'd better get ready for the games. I am going to check on Cozmo."

CHAPTER 20

I was still upset over the conversation with my friends. I walked down the hallway hoping to find Jett and Phoenix, but it seemed that Jett was about to get into a web of problems of his own.

Jett was primed and ready to compete in all the games. He was checking out some of his competition as they worked out in different rooms along the hallways.

Suddenly he came across Jezzica and Emily. It seems they were checking Jett out as well.

"Well, look who we have wondering the halls." Jezzica said as she seductively ran her long nailed hand up Jett's muscular arms and around his shoulder.

"Yes sister," said Emily as she came around his other side and grabbed his other arm and looked into his eyes. "Maybe we could be his personal tour guide and show him around the castle. We could show him all the different gyms we have for our guest to workout in before the competition. Not that you need to work out."

Emily and Jezzica kept rubbing their nails up and down his neck.

Jett shook the girls off his arms. "Trust me when I say, I don't need any help, especially your kind of help. You see, I like my blood where it is, in my body."

"Oh Jezz! Do you hear him? Jett thinks that we want to drink from him. Silly boy. We would never think of doing something like that," said Emily.

"Unless you ask or better yet beg us to," added Jezzica as she quickly turned his head toward her.

Jett quickly looked away and shook his head no.

"If you really want to help, you can tell me if you have seen my friend Phoenix. I have been looking for her."

At that moment Phoenix came from the other end of the hall. "Did I hear someone calling my name?" She asked. Phoenix circled Jett very closely pushing Jezzica and Emily out of the way. She gave Jett a big hug and then kept her arm around his shoulder and gave a cold death stare to Jezzica and Emily, warning them without a word to back off.

Then something weird happened to Jezzica and Emily. Their eyes turned completely white, and they just stood perfectly still as if they were frozen. After a minute their eyes returned to normal, and they looked at each other then back to Jett and Phoenix.

"Well, we need to be going anyway. It seems our fair Sorceress needs us," said Jezzica. She leaned over to Jett's ear and whispered, "Maybe next time it will be just you and me in the halls. Until then…"

Suddenly something even more bizarre happened. The girls raised their hands and pointed their nails towards their faces. A web-like substance shot out of their nails and covered their faces, followed by their bodies, until a webbed cocoon surrounded them. Then it fell to the ground and two black widowed spiders came out, climbed up the wall and into a vent.

"Did we just see what I saw?" asked Phoenix as she scratched her head.

"Yes we did, Phoenix," I said as I came around the other corner of the hall. Jezzica and Emily are known as SpiderVamps. They are a crossbreed. No one knows how they came about or how many of them there are, nor where they came from." I laughed and said, "It seems to me, Jett, that you are a very delicious fly in their web."

"Yes, Jett," added Phoenix in laughter as she grabbed my hand. "It seems like you got yourself all tangled up in their web of lust. What will you do?" Phoenix said

We walked down the corridor toward the arenas where the games were to take place.

"Will you two stop," said Jett.

He ran up between us and put his arms around our shoulders and we laughed and walked together. "So where are the others?"

"Don't worry they will meet us there," I said.

27

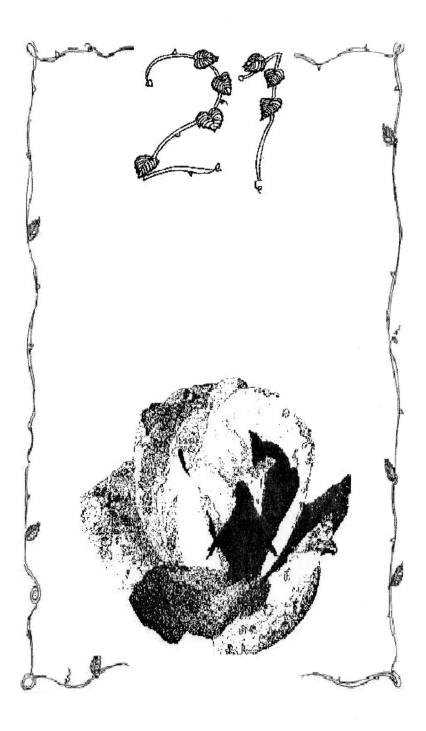

CHAPTER 21

While everyone in the castle was getting ready and heading down to where the games where to take place, Pheonna the Sorceress was in her room. She was looking into her magic pot and waiting for the spider sisters to come in.

The entered through one of the vents in her room, then they transformed back into their vampire bodies. "You summoned us my lady of evil," said Jezzica.

"You know I did. What took the two of you so long to get here?" Pheonna complained. "You were supposed to have reported back to me as soon as your horseback riding with Murranda was over. Why did you two morons take her to the prince? You know the more time they spend together the more likely he is to choose her as his queen. I am sure of it."

"Isn't there something more to it than that my lady?" Emily asked. "There are rumors about something even bigger than the prince wanting Murranda as his bride. There is something about her family that the prince is obsessed about."

"I know about the rumors that are going around. But that does not interest me right now. All I am concerned about is that I will one day marry the prince, and the two of us will rule side by side over the Shadow Land."

"I have an idea on how you can get what you want my lady," Jezzica said. "When one is obsessed with something or someone, just get rid of the obsession."

Jezzica looked at her sister with a fake loving look in her eyes. She was thinking about Jett.

"Maybe you have something there, Jezzica," Pheonna said as she looked into her magic bowl to see what Murranda and her friends were up to. "Maybe I need to find a way to remove her from my plans."

"But what about the rose she has?" Emily asked. "You see she has this special rose that is given to different people. It casts a shadow of Murry and shows the holder of the rose what Murry is doing. So how are you going to get rid of her without letting everyone with the rose know about it? We have no idea how many people have her rose."

"Somehow I need to get that rose or a seed of that rose so I can control what people see. You two go down to the games. Make sure that Murry and her friends stay there. If you see my sister, tell her I will be down as soon as I finish the surprise I have for her. Make sure that my sister also stays there. Do you understand? I am going to see if I can get one of Murry's roses or a seed. I will make my plans on how I will get rid of Murry once and for all before the end of the Masquerade Ball tonight."

The sisters transformed themselves back into black widow spiders and scurried up the wall and into the cracks of the room and headed down to where the games were to be held. They would keep an eye on Murry, her friends and Phoebe. But deep down the vamp sisters were just hoping to get a chance to see Jett and steal him away from the games…

CHAPTER 22

We arrived at the arena. Everyone was getting ready for the games to commence. In one area was the archery competition, in another were the sword fights, while others were competing using magic spells.

There was a water arena where mermaids competed in their own games. Above us in the sky were dragons, phoenixes and griffins competing in games of their own.

I couldn't wait to watch the games and also to sign up and try my hand at some. Jett, Phoenix and I started down to where people were signing up to participate. On our way, we ran into Nessa, Deena, Sky, Glitz, and Flutter.

Glitz spotted me first. "Hey Murry. There you are. We were wondering when you would get here. Deena was afraid you were with the prince again."

"Well I am here." I said looking over at Deena annoyed. "Deena needs to be enjoying the festivities like everyone else and not be constantly worrying about yours truly. So, have any of you signed up yet? Phoenix, Jett and I were just about to sign ourselves up for a few of these competitions."

"Are you sure you want to do that Murry?" Glitz asked worriedly. "You see most of the ones that are signing up for these competition events are trained warriors, hunters, and fighters. Don't you think you are out of your league? Aren't you worried you will get hurt?"

"Well. Thanks for the boost of confidence Glitz," I said sarcastically. "But no, I'm not worried. I am sure with all the training I received from Jett and

Nessa, in Elfinnia I can handle my own against these fighters."

I was anxious to sign up for the events, especially archery and sword fighting. Glitz and I watched some very skilled competitors. We saw knights and centaurs, and warrior elves fighting. We even saw Indians, vampires and werewolves. I had to ask myself how I, the daughter of a royal count who had never been away from home before, would be able to compete with these creatures.

"Let me guess. Someone is having doubts about her abilities." Jezzica said as she walked up to me in her spider form and then quickly webbed herself into her human form.

"Hello Jezzica. If you don't mind please get out of my head." I looked at her up and down with disgust."

"Aw Murranda! Why are you looking at me with such disdain? I thought we were becoming friends." She walked around me letting her long nails scrape gently against my shoulder.

"Well to be honest Jezzica, I don't know why. There is just something about you. Besides, I am not second-guessing my own skills. I am just becoming aware of how good everyone else is in these competitions."

"Maybe we can battle against each other in one of these matches. That is, if you're not too intimidated. But, I really want to go a few rounds with your elf friend Jett. He is more my speed." She licked her lips.

"Jezzica," I said with a grin. "I truly don't think Jett sees you in the way you see him. In fact I am sure he doesn't notice you at all. He seems to be getting closer and closer with Phoenix." I could see her blood boiling through her eyes as she watched Jett and Phoenix sparring and flirting with each other.

"So Jezz, about that challenge. I will take you up on it. Tell me when and where."

Just then a voice came over the speaker.

"Murranda and Jett please make your way to the archery area... You challenge will begin soon."

"Well, maybe next time" I said as I headed down to meet Jett "...and don't worry Jezz I'll be sure to tell Jett you said hello, *if* he remembers you..."

I hurried to the archery area where I found all my friends waiting on me. "I hope you don't mind," said Phoenix. "I signed you and Jett up for this. He told me that he and the other elves have been training you."

"Don't worry. I will take it easy on you Murry. I will even let you take the first shot nearer to the target." Jett said with a smirk as he handed me my quiver.

"Please don't do me any favors. I will be just fine and will shoot from where you shoot."

One of the prince's servants led us to our marks. On my right I saw our friend Phoebe and Prince Demitri up on a high balcony overlooking the tournament. But where was Pheonna?

Maybe she was heading up another challenge. So many were going on. Just then, Phoebe stood up and announce the rules.

"In this competition," began Phoebe in a loud commanding voice, "you have three archery challenges. The 1st challenge is to use all of your 10 arrows. If you reach the center of the bulls eye you get 50 points, outside of the center is 25 points outside of that is 10 points and outside of that is 5 points. After all 10 of your arrows have been shot, the one with the most points will win round one.

Each of you will take turns one at a time. Who will start this round?"

"Ladies first," said Jett. He was about to grab my arm and raise it, but I quickly grabbed and raised his instead. He was shocked and embarrassed.

"By all means, you go first." I said with a sinister chuckle and a wink.

All my friends laughed even Phoebe and the prince. "So be it!" said the prince. "The elf will take her mark. I mean *his* mark."

Jett took up his bow, aimed it and took the first shot. He was inches away from the bulls eye. Everyone clapped.

Now it was my turn. I was a little nervous, but I was not going to let him get the best of me.

I swung my bow off my shoulder and grabbed one of the arrows from my quiver, aiming directly for the target. I drew my bow back, closed my eyes and took a deep breath. I knew Jett was looking at me wondering why I had my eyes closed. I exhaled and let go. When I opened my eyes I knew I had the shot once I plucked my target

"BULLSEYE!" everyone yelled. My heart was racing so hard I thought it would come out of my chest.

"Lucky shot" Jett scowled, grabbing his next arrow from his quiver. He took aim and hit the bulls-eye leaving me the one with the "close" shot.

He walked past me and said, "See, it was only a lucky shot. Let someone with skills show you how it's done."

On our third target Jett hit the bulls eye again. So I stood where he had been, grabbed my arrow, aimed, closed my eyes and took a deep breath. Then I exhaled, opened one eye and took my shot. The arrow flew straight towards his and split his arrow in half. You could hear everyone gasp.

The crowd cheered with excitement. I looked over at Jett. I could tell he was not happy with me.

"Way to go Murry!" Sky yelled from the crowd. He had grown back to oversized and Hanna and Hymes Leadfoot were on his back.

Jett and I continued along the archery range. By the time we completed the tenth target, we were tied.

Phoebe stood up and calmed the crowd and began to explain the second challenge.

This time Jett and I would be on horses. We would ride until we found the six targets and aim for the bulls eye. Not only did we have to get a high score on target points but also on the fastest time.

It was my turn to go first and Deena volunteered to be my "horse." I grabbed my bow and arrow and mounted her, and took off looking for my targets.

As we waited for Phoebe to tell us to go, a voice came into my head *"Relax you've got this."* I looked around because the voice sounded so familiar. I was sure I had heard it before.

Then Phoebe said, "READY? GO!!!"

Deena and I took off. I saw the first target right away between two bushes. I quickly grabbed my arrow from the quiver and pulled back on the reins so Deena would know to slow down to a near stop. I let go of the reins grabbed my bow off my shoulder, aimed and quickly shot. I got the bulls eye. Then I quickly put the bow back around my shoulder, grabbed the reins and took off to the next target. The 2nd, 3rd 4th & 5th targets were easy to find. I hit the bulls eye each time. I was getting more and more excited.

Now the last target was all I had left. But where was it? I looked and looked around arena but couldn't find it. I was getting frustrated.

Something told me to look towards where the prince was sitting. The last target was beside him behind the dark castle flags. It was hidden pretty well but when I took a quick moment to collect my thoughts, I saw how the wind was blowing the flags around.

Deena quickly stopped so I could grab my bow and arrow and take my shot. I don't think anyone knew where that last target was. As I aimed everyone gasped and thought I was shooting at the prince. The guards took their positions to stop me.

Suddenly they realized what I shot as my last shot landed squarely in the middle of the target!

Now it was Jett's turn. As he grabbed one of the warrior elves' horses, I saw Phoenix run up to him and plant a big kiss for good luck. Just like me, he quickly found all the targets. His sixth target was easier to find since it was at the same place as mine had been. He too got all bulls eye. They measured each shot to see how close to the center we got on each of them, and I won. Everyone stood and cheered.

Then Phoebe stood up again and announced the third and final challenge.

"This time you will be on your horse and looking for your target as it moved around. There may be a deer on the run or a hawk in the sky. So you will need to look high and low and all around. You will do this at the same time. The one who reaches 12 objects first will WIN."

I was a bit confused about this challenge. Because this being the weekend of peace I thought we were not to kill anything. I leaned down to Deena and asked her about it. All she did was laugh. She said I was to do what I was told and I would see the outcome.

Jett and I started off side-by-side facing different directions. There was a rustle from a nearby bush. All of a sudden a raccoon came running out. We both shot at it. Jett hit it and once he did the raccoon burst into green smoke the same color green as his arrows were. Now I understood! They were not really live animals. They were some kind of illusion.

Now that I knew what was going on I was ready. Animals came from all around. The bushes, nearby trees, on the ground, in the air, and from behind the castle. So many were coming all at once, it was hard to figure out what to shoot.

Some we missed and others burst into colored smoked indicating a hit. I shot at a hawk that came from behind a statue, and a snake that was coming close to Jett's horse, but this shot scared his horse. It reared up and almost threw Jett off. He was not happy.

I looked at him and said, "sorry." He just looked back at me in a huff and continued to shoot.. 1, 2, 3, 4, 5, animals were shot. Our scores stayed even with each other.

Finally, we were tied at 11 each. One more kill and one of us would win the archery round. Then we saw it.

The final kill shot lay on the back of a Fiery Dragon. One minute it was made of fire then the next it was solid. I aimed ready to shoot just as Jett did. We both shot at the same time. We knew one of us had him. But we didn't.

When the arrows flew towards the dragon he turned into ball of fire and the arrows went right through him. He turned toward us and blew a huge ball of fire in our direction.

    Jett and I didn't know what to do. Nessa was just at the edge of our arena near a little pond. She swung her arms out in front of all of us. The water from the pond went into the forming a wall between us and the dragon. The ball of fire extinguished.

    We all were in shock!

    "How did I… What did I just do?" Nessa screamed. She looked at her hands and the water dropped back into the pond with a splash.

    Jett looked at his sister and said "Nessa you have the Gift!" Nessa quickly interrupted him and pointed at the dragon flying towards us.

    "Let's worry about your sister and what she can do later we have to finish this dragon somehow." I said, grabbing an arrow as quickly as I could to shoot.

    How can you shoot at something that can't be shot at? It did not make sense. But I was not going to give up and neither was Jett. Everyone was astonished by all of this, but no one more that Phoenix. The way she looked at that dragon it was almost as if she knew it.

    The longer Phoenix watched this fire dragon the more she changed. A fiery tattoo appeared and covered her body. Her hair kept growing, almost becoming like fire itself. Her skin kept getting redder and redder. She suddenly looked at herself changing and it scared her so much that she ran off into the woods. She left a small flaming trail that lasted a minute before dissipating.

    Jett and I continued shooting at the dragon. When we used all our arrows, the assistants brought us more. I soon noticed that whenever the dragon would turn into an actual dragon instead of a dragon shaped ball of flames, he couldn't spring over trees and things. Jett noticed too. We both knew what that meant.

We had to wait for that split second when the dragon became "solid" and then shoot at it. The next time he did, both Jett and I quickly drew back and shot. The dragon burst into a blue-green smoke, which meant we both hit him. We were tied again.

Everyone was cheering. I hopped off Deena while all my friends ran up to congratulate Jett and me. I ran to Jett to say "great job," but he was looking around for Phoenix.

He asked his sister where she had run off to. Nessa did not know. All she said was that Phoenix was acting very weird and had run off into the woods towards the lake. Jett ran after her to make sure she was okay.

He found Phoenix pacing back and forth by the lake seemingly talking to herself. Jett came up from behind Phoenix and put his hand on her shoulder. The moment he did she quickly grabbed his wrist and arm and flipped him across her shoulder several yards into a bush full of glittery flowers.

Once she realized it was Jett she ran to him. "Ooh Jett! I am so sorry. Are you okay? You scared me."

"I'm fine." He said as he picked himself up and dusted off all the glitter and petals. "I just came looking for you. You seemed uneasy when you saw the Fire Dragon. Is everything ok?"

"I'm okay, sort of, I don't know." she said with confusion in her voice. She quickly turned away from Jett and ran her fingers through her hair and twisted it. "I don't know how to explain this but it was as if moment I saw the fire dragon something weird was happening to me. My skin started to feel hot and was getting hotter the longer the dragon was fighting you and Murry. And when it looked like the dragon was going to win, I felt a rage. It frightened me. I felt as if I knew the dragon. Then there was one time when the dragon looked my way and seemed to recognize me. It smiled! That's when I ran."

"What are you talking about Phoenix. How could you possibly know a dragon?" Jett asked.

"I can't explain it Jett. It was just a feeling. I think I need to find these dragons to learn more. Haven't you noticed how I have been changing so quickly every day? This is not normal. You have to admit it. Once the weekend of peace is done and we have helped Murry find what she is looking for I must find The Cave of Dragons to get some answers. I don't want to leave you Jett. In case you hadn't noticed, I really do like you a lot. But I need to find my own answers. There is some kind of strong connection between the dragons and me. I can feel it."

"Well if you truly feel that way, you don't have to worry about leaving me Phoenix, because I am not going to let you do this alone. I will be with you. Because if you haven't noticed, I really like you a lot too," Jett said.

And then he kissed her.

23

CHAPTER 23

Once Jett consoled Phoenix they rejoined us at the tournament.

"Where have you two been?" I asked looking with suspicion at their guilt-ridden faces.

"I saw Phoenix run off to the lake and I ran after her to see if she was okay. I wanted to bring her back so she could be here when as announced ME THE WINNER of this archery competition." Jett said with a smug smirk on his face.

"Don't be so sure Jett. Who says YOU are the winner in this competition. I think it's clear to see that…."

"It's A TIE!" The Prince stood and announced. "This is the first time in the history of this land that we have had a TIE. Now what shall we do to break it and see who goes to the final round. I say we let both of them go and duel it at the finals. If you agree stand and cheer for the victors."

Once he said that the crowd got to their feet and all you could hear was "HAIL TO MURRANDA AND JETT! HURRAY! HURRAY."

Unbelievable! We would both go to the final round. We enjoyed watching other competitions as we waited our turn.

There were many different and unusual events such as fairies doing bug racing where surprisingly, Glitz and Flutter won. They won because as they got near the finish line Glitz got his ladybug's wing and the rein tangled up which caused most of the fairies to fall off their bugs as they tumbled toward the finish line.

Since Flutter and Glitz were still on their bugs at the end they won. I was both embarrassed and proud of them.

There were also other shape shifters and chameleons like Sky in a competition to see how fast they could blend into their surroundings. The winner would be the one who was not discovered. The twist was that their surroundings kept magically changing, and they have to see how fast they could change so they wouldn't be spotted. In this competition there was another TIE! It was between Sky and female chameleon shifter who was part leopard and part human.

Her name was Ashanti and she seemed quite smitten with Sky. Every time Sky looked her way she would blush and turn away. She was also quite beautiful. In human form she looked a lot like me, with long black hair. When she shifted, her fur was jet black with just a little dark fray around her leopard like ears and on the tip of her long tail. She had long nails that looked like claws and her eyes were as deep blue as the ocean. Her fur covered certain parts of her body but she also wore a leather top and pants that looked like they were painted on her.

There were events for everyone from giants to mermaids, from hobbits to trolls, from Pirates to Indians, from wizards to sorcerers, from vampires to werewolves, from fairies and elves and garden and wood nymphs – all could participate.

Some of the competitions were thrilling to watch while others were just plain funny, such as the Pirate's "man down" competition. The pirates as well as the hobbits and dwarves got in line in front of a table facing each other. They all drink shots of whiskey or rum and the last one standing was the winner. Each time one of them would pass out drunk, the crowd would yell, "Man Down Man Down."

The vampires and werewolves had to run an obstacle course. The vampires had to avoid getting staked or beheaded and had to stay away from sunrays. Because this was a friendly competition the sun was fake and instead of the stake going through the heart or the axe cutting off the head, a red mark would be placed on the chest or neck.

The werewolves had to go through their own obstacle course without getting hunted down. Instead of silver bullets, they would be hit with silver paint.

Mermaids had their own water obstacle course. They had to complete it without getting netted.

We could compete in as many events as we wanted. I chose several. I did not win every one I entered, but it was okay.

I heard my name being called out from among the crowd. It was the Prince. I went to where I was told to meet him.

"Hello," I said with a curious expression on my face. "What do you need from me?"

"Well this is a competition is it not?" He replied. "I signed us up for a sword fighting competition. Let's just say a little birdie told me you have been training for such a thing in case you were to come upon a battle. I'm quite curious to see how good you are. I promise to take it easy on you since I'm sure this is your first time." The prince said with wry smile.

I looked at him, grabbed my sword and quickly prepared myself. I then flicked off one of the emblems he wore on his cape's collar.

"Take it easy on me if you must your Majesty, but I won't be easy on you."

The servants came to adjust our swords by attaching a rubber tip with a light to the sharp tip so that whenever contact was made it would show a point in our favor. The one with the most points or the one that would pin the opponent was the winner.

"You don't mind that I signed you up with me?" Prince Demitri asked. "Signing us up made me feel… nostalgic. Your mother and I competed against each other the last time she was here. I am sure if you are anything like your parents you can probably hold your own."

I couldn't say anything. I just blushed and looked away. The moment I did that he swung his sword and flicked my hair almost hitting my cheek.

I quickly pulled my hair back as we walked up to the center of the arena. I looked around wondering why no one gave us the proper safety garb to wear. The Prince just looked at me a laughed.

"What, you can't fight the old fashion way. You need the protective gear. Maybe I was wrong about you."

I took my sword and drew a line in the ground. "Can we start this or are we just going to talk?" I said looking at him, annoyed.

We took our marks. Phoebe stood on the balcony stand and looked at both of us. I could tell from her expression that she was not happy the Prince and I were competing. I could see all of my friends near her looking at me as if they wanted to grab me out of the competition.

Phoebe put her hands in the air to silence the crowd. "Are the competitors ready?" We looked at her and nodded. "Face each other," she continued. "Ready? Fight!"

Clink! Clink! Our swords hit each other and little sparks flew from the edges. The prince lunged at me and I blocked and quickly turned. I would just as quickly lunge at him and hit his side.

"So, I see you have been practicing," he said as he kept lunging at me.

"Maybe just a little," I replied.

I kept my arms up, fending off his attacks. Each time the Prince lunged at me I could feel my friends' fears grow even more intense. This made me want to win even more to prove to my friends that I could take care of myself.

I could see out of the corner of my eye that Phoebe was looking at me. She seemed to be looking to make sure I was wearing the necklace she gave me.

I hoped she wouldn't realize that the stone in the necklace was not there.

On and on we fought, a point for him then a point for me; a jab and lunge here and a block and twist there. Then he made an unexpected move that caused my sword to fly out of my hand, and up to the balcony where Phoebe was standing. You could hear the crowd gasp.

I could see the fear in Phoebe's eyes. I ran to the wall behind the prince, climbed it, pushed off and flipped over his head grabbing my sword on the way down. I looked at Phoebe, winked and landed with a flip next to the prince.

I swung hard, knocking his sword out of his hands. Then I quickly swung my leg and knocked his feet from beneath him. I stood over the prince gripping the sword with both hands and pointed it over his heart.

I looked him square in his eyes expecting him to show fear. Instead Demitri just looked at me with surprise and pride.

Phoebe quickly stood up and yelled, "STOP! MATCH OVER! WINNER MURRANDA!" Everyone stood cheering, everyone except the other vampires and werewolves. They just hissed and hissed. I didn't really know how to take that.

I put my hand out for Demitri to grab. He took it, stood up and kissed the back of it with his cold breath. It immediately gave me goose bumps.

"Well done," he said. "Your mother and father would be proud of you. So should your friends, but most of all you should be proud of yourself." He winked at me. Suddenly I remembered the conversation we had the night he walked me to my room.

All I could do was smile and nod. I began thinking about my father. I knew he had to be getting close. He and Jeffery are still looking for me. I wonder where they are right now. Have they made it to the castle yet?

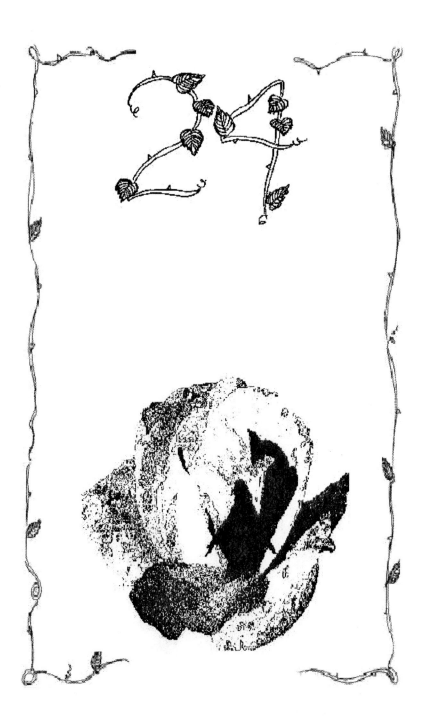

CHAPTER 24

While everyone at the dark castle was enjoying the competition during this weekend of peace, Murranda's father Rudolpho and his butler and best friend Jeffery continued to follow Phoebe's bird. Her friend Sheila had instructed them to follow the bird and it would lead them not only to Phoebe but also to Rudy's only daughter.

As they followed the bird hoping to find Murranda, Rudy held on to "The Murry Rose." When he saw in the rose that Murry was going into the Shadow Land he knew he had to go look for her before she got to close to the prince and found out the truth. Then when he saw her in some kind of competition with the prince, it did not set very well with him.

"Jeffery why aren't we there yet? Shouldn't we be at the castle by now?" He said with a very worried voice.

"Sir we haven't even passed through Elfinnia yet. Once we pass through there it will be no time at all before we reach the Shadow Land and the Dark Castle." After he said that the bird began whistling a familiar tune.

"Jeffery do you hear that?" Rudy asked with a surprised look. "The tune the bird is singing, I have heard that before. We must be close now. I remember the elves playing that same tune during one of their celebrations."

Rudy was right. The bird led them straight into Elfinnia where they came upon their old friend Evanwood.

"I could feel a familiar presence coming into our humble village," said Evanwood as he came down from one of the tall tree house. Phoebe's bird was sitting on his shoulder and he was gently petting its chest. "How are my old friends? I can see you have traveled far and still have a ways to go." They shook hands and sat on the wagon.

"I know my daughter was here and you took great care of her and for that I am grateful. But I know she is no longer here because she is in the Shadow Land. You must know that is a place I fear for my daughter's life, and it's why Jeffery and I are in search for her. I wish I could stay longer and catch up on old stories. You and the other elves have been friends with my family for years, and I know it has been a while since we have seen one another. Once I find my daughter I promise to come back this way and visit longer, but we must be on our way. Please understand old friend"

"I do understand my friend," Evanwood replied. "But have you forgotten that some of us can speak to animals and this bird is very tired and hungry just as your horses are. He must rest and so must your horses. I am not saying overnight, just a few hours for them to rest and have a bit of food. We have just prepared some food. We have plenty for you and Jeffery as well. Come let my elves take care of the bird and your horses."

"We cannot wait we MUST go!" Rudy said franticly "If we don't follow the bird we will find our own way. I must get to my daughter NOW."

Jeffery put his hand on Rudy's shoulder and said, "Sir, we must rest some and let the animals do the same. It's not far now, but if we don't get some rest you will not have the strength to face anyone. Also, we are out of supplies. So please sir your daughter is okay. It's the weekend of peace so the prince or anyone there wouldn't dare break the rules during this time."

"Jeffery is right old friend. Stay, eat and rest a bit. The rose shows that your daughter is fine. In fact, she is just participating in some friendly competition held during this time of peace. This custom has been going on for centuries." Evanwood helped his tired friends off their wagon.

"Okay, fine. We will eat and rest for a bit, but we must not stay long. I feel my daughter needs me," Rudy reluctantly agreed.

"Then come. We will feast."

Evanwood put his arms around his two friends' shoulders and led them to the feast. As they sat and ate, Evanwood spoke to them about the old days when Rudy and Jeffery and even Rudy's beloved Morinda would come visit during their travels. For a bit Rudy smiled and laughed seeming to enjoy himself, but deep down you knew he was still worried about Murranda.

Evanwood looked at Rudy and put a hand on his shoulder. "Old friend, if I can, I will get you to the castle sooner. If I cannot, just follow Phoebe's bird. It will lead you right to your daughter. First, will you do an old elf a favor? One thing I haven't told you is the real reason for this feast and why I asked you two to stay. This is the Feast of Passage. It's my time to pass through. My life on this plane of existence has come to an end."

"NO! Say it's not so!" Both Rudy and Jeffery said sadly. "What can we do old friend?" Rudy asked.

Evanwood grabbed Rudy's hand and laid down a crystal pebble and then closed his hand tightly. Rudy could feel his friend getting weaker by the moment.

His breathing had become shallow and he was getting paler and paler.

"Please find Nessa and Jett together and tell them of my passing. Make them promise they will stay with Murry on her journey. Let them know that that is my last request for them. Give Nessa the pebble and tell her that I know about her new gift. She and her brother are to find the nearest pond or lake and build a small fire near it. Then she is to use her powers to bring the fire and water together. That is where I will appear to them.

"Of course I will. I just wish there was something I could do so you wouldn't have to pass through. You have done so much for me and my beloved wife and family"

"And you have taught me so much. I know I can never repay you," added Jeffery.

"Well then," Evanwood said, "my elves will gather your horses and wagon and bird, of course, and bring them to the "Circle of Fire & Water" where we will meet them. Then you and your team will walk through it and you will be at the entrance of the Dark Castle where the tournaments are still going on. The Circle of Fire & Water is a secret place that elves use to travel through if they need to get somewhere that is far. Now this next thing I ask is going to be the hardest part for you as a father," Evan added.

"Find my elves first before you look for your daughter. They must know as soon as possible so they will know what to do next. Then you can find your daughter. I am sure they will know where Murry is and will take you to her."

As they listened to Evanwood speak they could tell he was about to pass. They quickly brought him to the "Circle of Fire & Water" where all the other elves gathered. It was where they held the ceremonial passing of the elves. The older elves would pass through to their next life's journey.

One of the other elf leaders came and took Evanwood to the gathering. One by one the elves approached him, kissing his hand or forehead. Each elf took a clear vial that was in his hand and put it to their cheek. A single tear would fall into the vial. The next to the oldest elf leader took the vial and placed it around Evanwood's neck and laid him on what looked like a bed of clouds hovering over the Lake of Tears.

The lake flowed down to a huge waterfall, the most beautiful one they had ever seen. It was clear blue with strings of gold flowing through it. The strings of gold were the tears of elves who had passed on before.

The new Wizard Elf helped put Evanwood on the cloud-like bed. He placed the vile of tears around his neck and onto his chest. They sent Evanwood to sail across the river and into the falls.

When he reached the edge, Evanwood magically became one with the river. For a brief moment the whole falls became golden. You could hear the faint sounds of a sad elf song. It was the saddest song ever heard. Sad it was, the passing of one meant the coming of another.

CHAPTER 25

Before Evanwood passed, he watched as Rudy and Jeffery climbed into their wagon. Rudy put the crystal water pebble into his upper pocket and held the Murry Rose as Jeffery grabbed hold of the reins. They looked back at the other elves and at Evanwood and without saying a word they sadly said their goodbyes to an old and dear friend knowing that one day when it was their time to pass they would see him once more.

They commanded the horses to go through the circle and as Evanwood predicted, the horses was very skittish going through the Circle of Fire & Water. Once the horses were calmed, they finally walked through the circle and just as Evanwood had said, Rudy and Jeffery found themselves standing in front of the entrance to the Dark Castle.

"We are here, Jeffery. Let's quickly find my daughter," Rudy said.

"Wait Sir!" Jeffery said. "Remember your promise to Evanwood. Have you forgotten that so quickly?"

Rudy jumped off the wagon, patted his upper pocket and looked at Jeffery. "You're right Jeffery. A promise is a promise. Let's go look for Nessa and Jett. It will be nice to see them again. I wish it were under better circumstances."

Rudy helped Jeffery tie the horses in front of the castle doors. Then they went looking for the two elves. Phoebe's bird was perched on Jeffery's shoulder in search of Phoebe.

As they reached the arena they could hear familiar voices. Jett and Nessa were talking about

Nessa's new powers. Rudy and Jeffery could see Nessa looking at her hands and trying to make something move the same way the water had. This time nothing happened.

Jeffery and Rudy yelled out to them. "Hey Nessa! Jett! Nessa! Jett!"

Nessa and Jett looked behind them and smiled. They ran to Rudy and Jeffery. They were so surprised to see them and not sure how to act knowing Murranda was there also in the arena.

"Count Rudolpho. Jeffery. How long has it been? How are you two? Why are you here?" Nessa said, looking around for Murry, but trying not to be too obvious.

"I am sure you know we are looking for my daughter Murranda. I know you and the others healed her from her last injury, and I am eternally grateful. But we are also here for another reason, a promise we made," Rudy said as he grabbed their hands. They looked into Rudy's eyes and they knew.

"When did Brother Evanwood pass?" asked Jett.

"Just before we came here. He helped us go through the Circle of Fire & Water so we could get here faster," Jeffery told them.

Jett was about to take off back to Elfinnia when Jeffery stopped him. With both hands on Jett's shoulders he said, "You both must stay and protect Murry during her journey. You must see her through it It is what he wants of you."

Jett just looked down in sadness as Rudy took Nessa aside to give her the pebble and told her what she needed to do with it.

"I don't know if I can," she said. "What I did with the water earlier only happened once. I have been trying to make it happen again ever since then but nothing happens."

"Evanwood had faith in you Nessa," said Rudy. "He wouldn't ask you to do something he did not think you could do. Trust in him. Go with your brother Jett and do what he has asked of you."

Nessa called for Jett and they walked to the nearest pond. Phoenix saw what was going on and ran to them.

"Are you okay?" She asked.

"Yes I am," he said. "But my sister and I have to do something. It must be just the two of us. Please understand and know I am okay. I will to you later."

Phoenix kissed Jett and let him and his sister go. They went to the nearest pond to build a small fire so Nessa could fulfill Evanwood's request.

"I don't think I can do this Brother," Nessa said with doubt in her voice.

"Concentrate little sister. But not with your head, with your heart. You were given this ability for a reason. Think of our brother and how much we want to see him and then bring the water to meet the fire just as he said. You can do this."

Nessa closed her eyes and thought of Evanwood and how much she missed him. She turned towards the water and fire and lifted her hands. Just like magic the water rose and so did the fire. She crossed her hands and both elements met in the middle and formed a wall of steam. As the wall formed so did an image of Evanwood.

"I knew you could do this sister," Evanwood said through the wall of steam. "Since you can see me here, I have already passed through to my next journey in life. Do not cry for me. As you both know, everything has a beginning and an end. Now this is the ending to my journey here, but I will always be with you."

Now I know you Jett," Evanwood said as he looked at his brother. "You are going to want to go back to Elfinnia and lead the other elves. But your place right now is here with Murry. Both of you must stay with her on her quest. Deep down you both know this to be true. Plus you have a mission of your own brother with your new friend Phoenix. Are you surprised I know about you two? I have my ways of watching over you all. I knew there was something different about Phoenix when she came to our land. I did not know that the two of you would get so close but I am happy for you. Something tells me she will be very beneficial to us all in the long run, once she finds out who she is and what she is capable of.

Sister dear, I know this new gift you have is very scary and you don't know how to control it now. But trust me, you will. You must look for one of the native Indians from the castle. He will know who you are and will be there to guide you and teach you how to use your new found gift. You will know him by his markings. He has all the elements on his arms, Earth, Fire, Wind, and Water. This new gift you have Sister will be of great use to help your friends and your brother. Jett, you will soon lead our elves as it has always been written. For now, do as I have asked. I promise I will be watching from beyond and guiding you both. Have faith my family. For there are bigger things waiting for you both, and your friends also. Be strong and brave and know I am always near." Evanwood disappeared into the mist.

Nessa put her arms down and the fire and water returned to their own spaces.

"I'm glad someone has faith in me," Nessa said as she scratched her head and wiped the tears from her eyes. "Who is this Indian I am supposed to look for? How could our brother leave us like this without telling us before we left on this journey with Murranda. I am sure he knew he was going to be passing before we started." She grabbed hold of Jett and cried on his shoulder.

Jett stroked her hair to help her calm down even though he too had tears in his eyes. He pulled himself together and said, "Now Nessa, we need to honor our brother's last wishes. I too don't understand why he made us leave when I'm sure he knew he was going to pass soon, But we still need to do what he asked of us. Evanwood was always the wisest of us all. So let's go sister and find this Indian and our friends. I am sure Murry is going to want to know about our brother also. Plus we need to help our old friends Rudy and Jeffery." Jett put his arms around his sister and walked back to where Rudy and Jeffery were waiting for them.

Nessa and Jett caught up with Rudy and Jeffery as they were looking around for Murranda. "Thank you for letting us know about our brother and for giving us the special pebble," Jett said as he shook their hands.

"Your brother will be greatly missed. Your clan has always been very important to my family." Rudy said as he took his other hand and placed it on Jett's shoulder as a sign of friendship.

"Sir Rudy is right," Jeffery agreed.

"Yes, he was the wisest of us all in Elfinnia. He was the one who brought peace between the realm of man and Elves," Nessa said with pride in her voice. "Let's go look for your daughter Rudy. But before we do…"

"WHAT NOW! What do I have to wait on NOW? I am worried for my daughter's safety," Rudy interrupted with anger.

"Rudy, please calm down. You need to know something first. It's about the Dark Prince," Nessa tried to continued.

"CALM DOWN? What do you mean calm down? Now you are telling me something about the prince and my only daughter and you think I can just stay calm? I knew I should not have allowed this crazy journey of hers. She doesn't even know what she is looking for and now she has ended up here. I am still not sure how she ended up here in the first place. I knew something like this would happen. I knew the prince would try to take my little girl. He has hurt her somehow and he wants to have a weekend of peace. He is a monster a blood-sucking monster. Where is he? Take me to him NOW so I can…" Rudy shouted as he started to run into the arena where all the competition was taking place.

Jett quickly got in front of Rudy and placed both of his hands on Rudy's shoulders to stop him from going any further. "WAIT RUDY! Let my sister finish what she is trying to explain to you."

"As I was saying," continued Nessa, "Murry and the prince have been spending a lot of time together despite what we have been telling her. And it seems that the prince has been telling her things that a lot of us haven't told her about her mother. I am sure you haven't as well. I do understand why, but Murry is very disillusioned now about you and Jeffery and all the stories that you told her in the past about her mother. I don't think the prince has told her WHO or WHAT her mother truly was, but Murry does know there is more to the story. She is not refusing to leave the castle until she knows the whole truth about Morinda."

While Nessa explained what had been going on between the Dark Prince and his daughter, Rudy's face turned a ghostly white. He was so frightened by what he was hearing, but at the same time he felt bad for keeping things like this from his only child. He only did it out of love for his little girl.

He had his reason. In part it was because of what his beloved wife Morinda asked of him before she died, and also because he was afraid of what might happen if she knew. He had already lost his Morinda, he did not want to also lose his only child. She was the last connection he had to his beloved wife.

Now that the prince was slowly revealing who she was and where she truly came from, he needed to get to his daughter as soon as possible so he could explain everything.

"She needs to hear the whole truth from me, her father." Rudy said frantically.

"Right now she is in a competition with the prince," said Jett. "They are sword fighting, and she is doing very well."

"WHAT? Are you kidding me?" He was even more worried about his daughter now.

"Rudy, you truly have nothing to fear. Not only is this the weekend of peace but all they are doing is participating in the friendly competitions that are held before the big Masquerade Ball," Nessa said as she tried to calm Rudy down.

"Plus your daughter can fight," Jett said mimicking sword movements with his arms. "When she and her friends were staying in our land we taught her how to sword fight as well as other self-defense strategies such as archery and hand-to-hand combat," Jett said. "She picked up on it all very quickly."

"Well, she is a quick learner Sir." Jeffery added as he put his hand on Rudy's shoulder. "Remember, she was your top student when you taught fencing back home."

"I know," said Rudy. "But as a father you never want to see your daughter in any kind of combat. I can't help but worry about her. You will all know this if and when you have children of your own. Now, please I will ask one last time, take me to my daughter now or I will look for her myself. I did what Evanwood asked of me, now it's time to help me as promised and find my daughter so I can take her away from here and from the prince. No more stalling. She may not be happy to see me right now after what the prince has told her, but that is the least of my worries. Please let's go."

Nessa and Jett looked into Rudy's desperate eyes and nodded in agreement. Jett, Nessa, Jeffery, and Rudy ventured out with Phoebe's bird still resting on Jeffery's shoulder. They made their way into the arena, scanning the crowd for Murry.

CHAPTER 26

After my victorious match with Prince Demitri, Deena, Glitz, Flutter, Phoenix and Sky all ran up to me and gave me a huge hug while at the same time pulling me away from the prince.

"Where did you learn that move, Murry?" Glitz asked with surprise in his voice while Flutter signed the same thing. None of my friends could believe how I beat the Prince. But to tell you the truth, neither could I.

"I don't really know." I replied, looking for the Demitri. "It was just instinct. When I saw where my sword had landed I just knew what to do."

I finally spotted the prince among the other vampires and creatures. They were looking him over to see if he was okay and looking at me, hissing.

He instructed them not to be angry at me as I had won fairly. That did not sit well with them nor did it sit well with Pheonna.

When I looked over at Phoebe I saw her sister sitting next to her fuming while Phoebe was smiling at me with such pride. Then her face changed into confusion.

She had looked up at bird flying towards her and now hovering beside her. She put her hand out for it to perch. Then I saw her looking around, but for what I didn't know.

I felt something cold touch my right arm and move down slowly to my hand. When I looked around I saw Demitri standing there trying to pull me away from my friends. Flutter pushed herself between us and began frantically signing. I understood the word "no."

I was surprised at Flutter's boldness, but what really surprised me was when Demitri signed back to her saying, "I am sorry but she needs to come with me so we can get ready for the final round to see who is going to be the ultimate grand winner of the Golden Owl?"

The golden owl Cozmo, I had almost forgotten about him. I hope the prince meant what he said about making a duplicate of our friend when all this competition was over. Then they would let Cozmo go free, even though Cozmo did bring this upon himself by his own greediness.

Flutter just looked down at the prince and signed, "Okay, but as soon as it's over we get her. Deal?"

Demitri nodded his head in agreement. As the prince pulled me away from my friends, I told them I would be right back. I know they were not happy that I went off with the prince again.

"I'm sorry for taking you away from all that praising from your admirers," Demitri said. We began walking away from the crowds and towards the back of the arena and the area for the royals.

It was a huge tent with lots of silk and velvet pillows in all the royal colors. The servants were pouring wine and juices for the royals. They were serving all kinds of exotic fruits, cheeses, breads, and meats.

"That's okay," I said as he led me in. "But I have to say I am quite impressed that you know how to talk to Flutter. I didn't know you knew how to sign."

"Well, as a prince I am required to know many different languages and that is one of them. I am sure since your father is a Count for the Royal King and Queen of your realm that he too knows many languages."

He was right my father did. I am sure he even knew sign language. *I just wished I did*, I thought. "If you truly desire to know how to sign I am sure you will learn. And I am sure it will come easy to you just as other things have."

He was right again. I was a quick learner on many things. I surprise myself a lot of times.

"I just wish I knew how to sign now while we are all here," I said looking down with disappointment in my voice.

"But you can Murry. You just need to truly desire it and you will know how." Demitri said. I knew he was reading my thoughts again. But what did he mean by that? How can I learn something just by simply desiring it so? "Try It." Demitri said.

"How?" I asked.

"Before you say or think of anything else," desire with all your heart the knowledge to know how to talk to your friend Flutter. Then sign to me the very next thing that comes to your head."

So I did. I could feel my heart racing with the desire to know how to communicate with my dear friend Flutter. Then I looked up at Demitri and signed, "Okay how? What do I do it? I have the desire but how can I--I--I ..." Then I looked at what I was doing. Not believing what I was seeing. "How is this happening? How do I know this so quickly when this weekend was the first time I had seen anyone using this language? How can I already know how?"

Demitri just looked at me and smiled. "Don't worry about how you know this. Just be glad that you can now talk to your friend. All your questions will be answered when it's time. You are so much more than you realize Murry and you are so much like your mother. It seems you two have the same gifts, but something tells me there is even more to you than even I know."

What did he mean by that I thought to myself. This time he didn't respond to what I was thinking. I am sure it was because he knows I hate it when he and my friends read my thoughts.

I couldn't help but think there were even MORE SECRETS being kept from me. Perhaps he just meant that my mother and I were both quick to learn new things. But, how could I possibly learn to sign so quickly when this weekend was the first time I ever seen someone using sign language.

Demitri led me to a quiet corner where we could be alone. He sat me down around some of the big silk and velvet pillows and summoned one of the servants to come pour me something to drink. "What would you like?" he asked.

"Any kind of juice would be fine." I said.

"What? No wine? We have the finest wine in the land."

"No thank you. I might want to participate in another contest, so I better keep my wits about me." I said with a giggle. Both the Prince and the servant nodded in agreement and also laughed.

She poured me some juice and gave the prince what looked like a very dark red wine, but slightly thicker. I knew what it was. I just shook my head.

"Does this bother you?" He asked as he took a quick sip and looked at my expression of disgust.

"Not really," I said. "I just keep forgetting that not only are you the Dark Prince, you are also…"

"A VAMPIRE!" We both said in unison. I quickly looked away as my face was turning red.

He placed one cold finger on my chin and turned my face towards his. "You are not afraid of me are you? Knowing what I am?"

"I should be I guess, but I'm not." I replied as I smiled and looked deep into his very icy blue eyes. I couldn't help myself. He had a magnetic way about him.

He leaned onto the pillows drinking his blood and looking at me with those deep ghostly, icy blue eyes.

"I have to say it again. When you ran up that wall behind me and flipped over to get your sword I was quite impressed, and I am a very hard person to impress. You remind me of your mother so much. It makes me miss her."

"Were you two close?" I asked with concern.

"Not like you may be thinking," he replied. "The only love your mother truly had was your father. But in a way I think we shared something special. I know she would be proud of the woman you have grown up to be Murranda."

He gently grabbed one of my hands. "You have her fearless quick thinking. I am somewhat surprised that you know so little about your mother. But then again I am sure your father had reasons for not telling you her whole story."

I drank my juice and slammed it down on the small table between us. "Uhh! My Father!" I said angrily. I folded my arms across my chest and let out a huff. "Demitri, from the things you have told me about my mother it seems my father has kept everything from me. His stories have been nothing but fantasies designed to put a child to sleep. I thought my father and I were so close. I didn't think we kept things from each other. But now I feel like I don't even know him. There is this huge secret between us."

Just then tears stared to fall. I was so hurt that he kept all this from me for all these years. Why?

Demitri stood up and put his arms around me to comfort me. "Don't be mad at your father. Soon you will have a chance to hear him out." He said as he held me close and stroked my hair."I did not mean to come between you and your father. You know this don't you?"

"I know."

Our faces were so close that I could feel his cold breath on my face. Our noses were just barely touching. The tension between the two of us was electric. But was it real? Was I having these strange close feelings towards Demitri because I felt he was the only one telling me the truth about my mother or was it more? I could see in his eyes he was feeling something as well. Was it the same as me? But then again what was I feeling?.

"Murranda!"

I felt someone grab my arm and pull me away from Demitri.

It was my father! He pushed me away and got right in front of the prince's face. He had a large silver dagger pressed against his pale white throat.

"You unhand my child! Just because you did not have your way with my beloved wife does not mean you can have my only daughter. I don't care what you predicted the last time. I told you once and I will tell you again Your Majesty..." My father said as he pressed the knife closer to his throat. "My family will NEVER be a part of yours! My wife did not become your bride and neither will my daughter!"

Bride? What was my father ranting about! Jeffery tried to hold me back as I tried to run to the prince. I thought my father was going to kill him. For some reason I did not want that to happen. I was very aware of what it meant to save a vampire, but at this moment he was my friend.

"Lady Murranda I think you need to stay with me here," Jeffery said grabbing my shoulders. "Your father has needed to do this for a long time."

I looked at Jeffery with pure shock. "Not you too, Jeffery. You have been keeping secrets from me as well? WHY?"

The prince quickly looked over my way as if to assure me that everything would be okay. I don't know why I wanted to protect him from my father but something inside me did. Once I saw the prince's expression I backed down.

'Don't you dare look over at my daughter!" My father yelled. "As I said before, my daughter will never be a part of your prophecy as long as I live."

"Well we can fix that!" yelled one of the prince's servants. She appeared from nowhere in a cloud of smoke behind my father. She grabbed him by the back of his neck, prepared to sink her teeth into him.

Demitri eyed at the servant warning her to back off. She quickly let go of my father, looking down with a shameful expression, then vanished just as quickly as she appeared.

"You are very lucky this is the weekend of peace, but you lay one more hand on my daughter and I'll be damned about any kind of peace." Father said without a single twitch.

Demitri stared into my father's eyes then with his left hand he took the end of the dagger and stuck it into the middle of his hand, pressing down the blade towards the handle. The blood began staining his white glove.

The dagger not only cut into, but went through to the back of his hand. "I understand your concern for your daughter old friend," Demitri said as he wiped off his hand once the dagger had completely vanished.

"I am not your friend!" My father said as he walked backwards towards me keeping his eyes on the prince. "And neither is my daughter." He added as he put his arms around me.

"Isn't that up to me father, who is or is not my friend?" I said. I quickly pulled away from Jeffery and ran to Demitri.

"Sunshine, you don't know this man if that is what I can truly call him, not like I do." Father tried to reach out to me.

"Maybe not since you failed to tell me that you had ever set foot into the Shadow Land, you or mother. Why is that father? Why keep things like that from me? Were any of the stories you told me even true? I feel there is something about my mother you don't want me to know, and I can't for the life of me understand why," I said with tears in my eyes.

The prince placed his hand on my shoulder to calm me."Murranda, I am sure your father and Jeffery had their reasons. Don't be too mad at them my dear."

"Murry, listen to your father," Jett and Nessa said as they ran between my father and me. "Rudy and Jeffery had valid reasons for keeping the truth from you."

Nessa tried to grab my hand and pull me away from the prince.

I quickly snatched my hand away from her. "Not you too, Nessa, Jett. Please don't tell me you both know something about my family that you have failed to mention. Who else knows?" I asked.

Part of me did not want to know the answer to that question.

"Your friends are right my dear," said Pheonna as she came out of the shadows. "Your family and friends had their reasons I'm sure. The prophecy they are trying not to speak of is…"

"Stay out of it Pheonna!" Demitri. She quickly put her hands over her mouth and looked at him with a not so innocent bat of her eyes.

"Prophecy? What prophecy? What is everyone talking about?" I asked looking around confused and dismayed.

I looked up at the prince and asked, "Can you get me out of here please? I can't take anymore of this. In fact I am done playing in the competitions. I know you wanted to spend time out here seeing me compete, but after all this I am trying to wrap my head around, I just need time to myself to sort it out. Please understand."

I looked back at everyone particularly my father, "And please, if you care about me and love me as you claim, let me have this moment to myself and don't come looking for me. I will find you all when I am ready to talk. I promise. I will be back before the Masquerade Ball.".

"But Sunshine, I was hoping to take you back home so I could explain everything to you. I promise to tell you everything. No more secrets, I swear. Please just come back home with me."

"Father I am sure you mean well. But you and Jeffery…" I tried looking at him with understanding yet disappointed eyes.

"It seems that everyone tries to mean well when it comes to my well being, but this is my life and my journey. I attend to finish and see it through. That means staying here through the Weekend of Peace Celebration, and heading back out on my journey afterwards. Besides, I have never been to a real ball. This time I WILL be attending. "

"Will you allow me to be your escort" the prince said as he carefully grabbed my hand.

"We will escort her to the Ball," said the rest of my friends as they came running to my side.

"No I will escort my daughter to the Ball," father said with a firm voice as he approached the prince and I.

"Father," I said as I held my arm out to stop him from coming any further. "I think I am old enough to decide who will escort me to my first ball."

I looked back at the prince and said, "Yes, you may escort me to the Ball. I would like that very much." The Prince took his cape and quickly wrapped it around the two of us.

Before anyone could yell "STOP!" Demitri and I vanished from sight. My father fell to his knees with tears in his eyes. Then all I saw was smoke.

I didn't know where the prince was taking me but I felt safe and did not care. I just needed to get away from all of THAT. I knew in my heart I was safe and that Demitri wouldn't hurt me.

27

CHAPTER 27

After Demitri and I vanished, Rudy stood up and looked all around with confusion and worry on his face.

"Where the hell did they go? Where did that Vamp Prince take my daughter?" There was anger in his voice and tears in his eyes.

Everyone rushed to his side to try and calm him. They told him how the Prince would surely not hurt me. Especially now, during this weekend of peace. She is safe they told him. But that was no comfort to Rudy.

"How can you be so sure? "I wouldn't put anything past that so- called prince no matter Peace or no Peace."

"Trust me, Sir Rudy," Pheonna said as she walked toward them. She was wearing a dark shimmering blue/black flowing dress with a long flowing cape with razor sharp points. She was holding her staff. It looked somewhat different than before, as if it had grown horns and the crystals glowed in different darker colors.

"My Prince wouldn't dare hurt your precious daughter. He has grown quite fond of her. I know you are worried because of the prophecy, but surely nothing will happen during this wonderful celebration. Let us all go back and enjoy. I am sure your daughter will come looking for you when she has settled down. Jett," she said, pointing to the elf, "I believe you have another competition with your friend Phoenix and two of my apprentices. I'm sure you have met Jezzica and Emily."

The mere mention of the Spider Vamps, made Jett's skin crawl, but when he heard Phoenix's name he was quite excited . He ran to the arena to meet her.

"I hate to admit this, but she is right," Sky said to Rudy and Jeffery. "There is nothing we can do now, and the prince is not going to hurt her. Let's just go back to the arena. We will find her I'm sure before the Ball begins. Maybe she'll find us during the Golden Owl ceremony."

"Oh! Wait! I remember seeing you in our Murry rose. You were with Lady Murranda when she fell into the trap near the gypsy fair. You helped her escape." Jeffery said as he approached Sky.

Sky nodded. Jeffery gave Sky a pat on the back.

"Sir," Jeffery added. "They are right. Let's just stay and look around. Maybe we can find out from others exactly how much of the truth Lady Murranda knows. Maybe even find our old friend Phoebe. I am sure you would like to talk to her to make sure young madam is wearing both the necklace and the ring. I am sure they are the same ones she gave your beloved Morinda when you two were on your last journey together.

Rudy picked up the pot carrying The Murry Rose in it and held it close to his chest. He then looked around and reluctantly followed everyone back to the arena hoping to find his little girl. He wanted to explain everything to her, but most of all to get her far away from the Prince and the Prophecy.

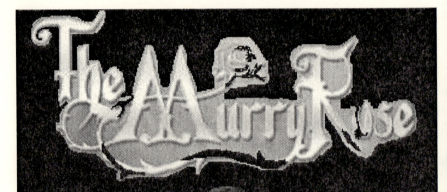

Here is a sneak peak of Part II of The Murry Rose series

After Murranda confronts her father and friends about all the secrets they have been keeping, she and the Prince pull a vanishing act.

Murranda's friends convince Rudy to not worry, reminding him this is the weekend of peace. They assure him that his daughter is fine and that he will see her before the Masquerade Ball later that evening. Meanwhile, they all return to the arena where the competition was continuing—the next: the SpiderVamp sisters against Jett the Elf and Phoenix.

While everyone is heading back, Pheonna the evil sorceress goes to her balcony where she intends to view the games. Following her was two little black spiders. The spiders transformed into the SpiderVamp sisters. The sisters listen as Pheonna makes plans for Murry's demise. With everyone at the competition, the sorceress arranges to have Murry kidnapped by pirates.

"Did you hear all that sorceress? It seems our little Murranda is having doubts about everyone. Finding out who she can and cannot trust" Jezz said, started tapping her long fingernails together with an evil look in her eyes.

"That maybe true" Pheonna said "but the more doubts she has against her family and friends the closer it seems she is getting to our Prince..."

"But that is good is it not? The closer she gets to the Prince, the closer we get to our prophesy." Emily said with a gleam in her eyes.

"Perhaps" Pheonna quickly replied "But I should be the one sitting by his side as Queen."

"But we thought after you found a way of getting

her here to the castle it was to ensure that the prophesy WILL come to pass" Jezz said with confusion in her voice.

"I did" Pheonna answered, "when I thought he was going to just use her up and get rid I her. But I can see that there is more to the two of them then even they realize. And I can't have that," she said slamming her staff on the ground. The sisters looked at each other in fear and confusion.

"So I am hoping my next plan will solve my little problem," the sorceress continued.

"What is that?" The sisters asked.

Pheonna grinned devilishly, "Let's just say that after our Dear Sweet Murry attends her first Masquerade Ball, you may just see a different side of her. Now don't you two have a competition to get to. You don't want to keep the Elf and his fiery little friend waiting now do you?" The sister returned sinister smirks and scurried their way back to the arena.

To be continued... Follow The Murry Rose series. "The Forbidden Rose" coming soon...

ABOUT THE AUTHOR

    C. H. Fortenberry lives with her husband in Chattahoochee Hills, GA. She has always had a vivid imagination and a story to tell. As a young person, she kept a journal beside her bed and recorded her thoughts and dreams. *The Murry Rose* evolved 19 years ago when she was pregnant with her son. Earlier in her life, in the second grade, she was diagnosed with dyslexia. Difficulty in reading and making out letters and proper placement became a great challenge into adulthood. She remained determined to not let her uniqueness deter her. After graduating from high school she attended a Junior College to study Sign Language.

    Her confidence began to build as she served as an interpreter for the deaf in local churches. She found a calling was reminded of her purpose, the creation and production of "her fantasy" writing a book to defy all of the odds. With a strong support system of friends, family, coworkers and especially her husband and son, she decided to finish what was started years ago—*The Murry Rose*. Her hope is that her story will motivate others with disabilities to follow their dreams. Speak your Success into Existence and let the Journey take you far!